1

'A talent to keep an eye on.' - Eric S. Brown, author of Bigfoot War

'A top-notch, thrilling read. Craig Saunders is a master of the genre.' - Iain Rob Wright, author of Animal Kingdom and Final Winter

'An awesome talent!' - Ian Woodhead, author of Shades Of Green and Infected Bodies

'The Love Of The Dead starts out like the typical horror novel you think you've read before, then whacks you over the head and goes in a direction you didn't see coming – think chainsaws at a daycare centre. Saunders' writing will creep into your spine and paralyse you with fear.' - David Bernstein, author of Amongst The Dead and Tears Of No Return

[The Love Of The Dead] 'Craig Saunders' unique chiller kept my eyes glued to the pages in anticipation.' - Kenneth Cain, author of These Tresspasses

'The boogeymen that inhabit the pages of Scarecrow & The Madness come from no supernatural plane of existence. Instead they come from the scariest place on earth: the human mind. These tales take place in our world with no hint of assistance from otherworldly forces, which is what makes them both so wonderfully diabolical.' - Patrick D'Orazio, author of The Dark Trilogy

'Scarecrow & The Madness is a wonderful hybrid approach to publishing; the print version of one of those creature double-features I recall so fondly from my youth.' - Gregory L. Norris, author of The Q Guide To Buffy The Vampire Slayer

'Anyone that has read Craig Saunders knows that his words flow like blood from a severed jugular. The Love Of The Dead is no exception. This book is all horror, though it will entertain any fan of detective mystery stories. Do yourself a favor and get this book. Read it, and then find Craig's other books and read them.' - Robert Essig, author of Through Hell, the Inbetween Awaits

'Rain is a dark, disturbing and violent supernatural horror novel with superb moments of suspense and terror.' - Travis L. Barrett, author of The Night Library

2

Also by Craig Saunders

The Walls Of Madness (Crowded Quarantine Publications)

Rain (Crowded Quarantine Publications)

The Love Of The Dead (Evil Jester Press)

A Stranger's Grave (Grand Mal Press)

Spiggot (Grand Mal Press)

Scarecrow And The Madness – with Robert Essig (Blood Bound Books)

Available exclusively to Kindle

NOVELS

Vigil: Vampire Apocalypse

The Seven Point Star

Evolution

The Outlaw King (The Line Of Kings Book One)

The Thief King (The Line Of Kings Book Two)

The Queen Of Thieves (The Line Of Kings Book Three)

Rythe Awakes (The Rythe Trilogy Book One)

Tides Of Rythe (The Rythe Trilogy Book Two)

The Line Of Kings Trilogy Boxset

COLLECTIONS

Dead In The Trunk

The Black And White Box

Coming Soon

Dead Boy: A Dead Days Novella (Grand Mal Press)

Rythe In Chaos (The Rythe Trilogy Book Three)

A HOME
BY THE SEA

CRAIG SAUNDERS

Printed And Bound in the United Kingdom
Crowded Quarantine Publications

A CIP catalogue record for this book
is available from the British Library

ISBN 978-0-9573999-2-1

Printed and bound in Great Britain
Crowded Quarantine Publications
34 Cheviot Road
Wolverhampton
West Midlands
WV2 2HD

This is a book about love. I'd like to dedicate it, too, to the people I love. Long, long, overdue.

My wife. My kids. My mum.

My nan and granddad. I think they'd get a kick out of this writing thing I seem to have got myself into.

And, now, the overdue bit...

There really are too many people to name individually, but this is for my Facebook friends. They've helped me through hard times, fun times, tough books and easy books. I write these books alone, but I'm never alone.

Finally, for Adam and Zoe-Ray Millard, who took a chance on these little books of mine.

The tide rises, the tide falls,
The twilight darkens, the curlew calls;
Along the sea-sands damp and brown
The traveler hastens toward the town,
And the tide rises, the tide falls.

Darkness settles on roofs and walls,
But the sea, the sea in darkness calls;
The little waves, with their soft, white hands
Efface the footprints in the sands,
And the tide rises, the tide falls.

The morning breaks; the steeds in their stalls
Stamp and neigh, as the hostler calls;
The day returns, but nevermore
Returns the traveler to the shore.
And the tide rises, the tide falls.

The Tide Rises, The Tide Falls
Henry Wadsworth Longfellow

PART ONE
THE MANNEQUIN

Irene Jacobs. She rolled it around on her tongue. Tried it out for size.

'Irene. Jacobs. Irene Jacobs.'

She shook her head. It didn't sound right. Irene Harris...Irene Jacobs.

'Sleep on it, Honey,' her mother said.

She did.

*

Irene always wanted a home by the sea. Somewhere to call her own, maybe a place with a view of the sea. Somewhere she was able to hear the waves rubbing the sand, or even just to get that fresh salt smell in her washing on a fine day.

She sat on the porch, hands on her belly, smiling.

She was petite and beautiful in a kind of boyish way. She was also young, and frightened. Her belly seemed enormous on her small frame, and so it should, because she was pregnant with twins.

She rubbed her belly and made a noise like the sand rolling in the tide, soothing her babies. One kicked and set the other off and she laughed.

Out here, way out on the point, with nothing to look at but the sea, she could think. She could feel.

Some people called it the spit, but she could never think of it like that. It was the 'point' to her, pointing out to sea, telling her to look and never forget, every single

11

day.

She was drawn to the sea. Always had been. When the Blue House came along she fell in love all over again, with that electric, sickening pulse deep within that couldn't be ignored. She'd had to have it.

Back in her old town, she hadn't been able to see clearly through the traffic, the Saturday shoppers, the queues at the supermarket and drunks walking past her door from the pubs further on down the street, singing football chants and swearing and fighting. Walking past dead kebabs that littered the streets and hearing the rumble of buses, or the plastic fake glass being smashed in telephone boxes. It was never the worst place in the country, or even the county, Norfolk, but something never felt right, like she didn't belong and was just a traveller, passing through.

The Blue House was right. She wasn't a traveller anymore. She was home.

The point ran slowly curving out to sea from east to west, joining the land in the east and petering out into the sea in the west. Out to the west was a seal sanctuary and on a still day she could hear them barking. The gulls and terns woke her first thing in the morning, as soon as the sky got light. They nested in the dunes that ran down to the beach. There were no trees, just hillocks with tufts of sea grass, lumps of driftwood and broken plastic and squid and broken nets and cages pushed up on the shore.

She could sit out on the sand or in the warm, like now, when it was autumn and that bite was in the breeze that you only got on the chilly Norfolk coasts.

To wake and walk down to the shore first thing in the

morning had become a ritual, no matter if it was blustery or warm or wet or cloudy. To look out at the weather way off over the rough North Sea, and know that Holland lay over the horizon in the north, and Norfolk and the whole of southern England at her back.

Every morning she stared with pale blue eyes at the sea, with the pale Blue House at her back and when she went back over the dunes to her home, she was never sad to leave the sea behind, because out on the point she was surrounded by it. From every room in the house she could see it. It was always there, when she woke and when she went to sleep. She could close her windows and shut out the sound of the waves breaking, but she never had.

Maybe the Blue House could save her. Let her be a mother to her children, concentrate on raising a family, and forget.

She smiled again, cooed, and her kicking babies calmed.

She wished Paul could have shared those kicks with her and held his big hands against her belly. She would have loved the chance to share the Blue House and the sea with the only man she'd ever truly loved. But he was gone and her babies were all she had left of him.

*

Marc Jones frowned and rubbed a hand through his unruly greying hair, looking at the delivery he'd just received. The offending article stood in the middle of the shop, Beautiful Brides. It wasn't what he'd ordered at all.

'What is that?'

The delivery man shrugged.

'It looks like a mannequin to me.'

'I know it's a mannequin. I ordered a mannequin. A dress maker's mannequin. I did not order *that*. It's...' Marc shook his head. He wanted to say it was a piece of shit, but he didn't like swearing unnecessarily.

It was a piece of shit, though, he thought.

The delivery man shrugged again. He couldn't give a shit either way. He had three more jobs on his docket, and he had to go half the way across the county from Blakeney to Yarmouth, out on the east coast of Norfolk, for his final run. He wouldn't be home 'til after seven as it was. He just wanted a signature.

'Sign here,' he said, holding out his electronic pad.

Marc shook his head. 'I'm not signing for it.'

'What am I supposed to do with it?'

'Take it back,' said Marc, mentally preparing himself for a battle of words.

'I can't take it back. I'm just here to deliver it. I'm the driver. You need to call whoever you ordered it from.'

'I'm not taking it, and I'm not signing for it,' said Marc.

The delivery man sighed. He closed his eyes and shook his head, like a man on the edge, counting to ten and thinking of balloons or Mickey Mouse, maybe, instead of lashing out with words.

'Look, Sir...' he said.

'No, you look,' said Marc, through gritted teeth. 'That thing's moth eaten. It's mildewed. It stinks, for Christ's

14

sake. It smells like dead fish or something.'

'It's not up to me, OK?'

'Just put it back on the van. I wasn't in, OK?'

The delivery man looked down at his feet. He really did want to be home early. He shook his head once again and picked up the mannequin.

'Whatever,' he said, and lumped it back out of the door of Beautiful Brides.

Marc puffed out some air, shook his head.

'For Christ's sake,' he said again.

*

The delivery driver lugged the heavy thing back out to the van and hefted it into the back, swearing a little under his breath, but not cursing too heavily.

He rolled a tight little cigarette. He wasn't allowed to smoke in the van, so he stepped round the back of the shop. Took a piss against the rear wall of Beautiful Brides, zipped up and nodded.

He finished his cigarette and returned to the van. The keys weren't in his pocket. They weren't in the driver's seat.

Something stank, stank like rotted meat. He turned his nose up and swore, more heavily this time, because if he'd lost the keys to the van there would be hell to pay from his boss and he'd never make it home for tea.

With a steadily darkening face he walked around to the back of the van and saw the keys swinging in the van's back door.

The delivery man laughed, shook his head, and took

his keys from the lock.

He wound down the window on the drive out and kept it that way for the whole journey to Yarmouth, because he just couldn't seem to get that stink out.

He never did notice the footsteps leading up to the van.

*

Marc went into the back of the shop and sat at his desk in the small office. The desk looked cluttered, but Marc knew exactly where everything was. The desktop screen on his PC was covered in files, accounting and letters, but there was order there, should someone bother to figure out what the system was.

The phone was under a note to make a call to a supplier. He moved the note aside and picked up the phone and dialled Irene's mobile from memory.

Reception was patchy at best out on the point, but the phone rang. Irene picked it up on the third ring. She must have had it in her pocket. Things must be getting hairy for her now, out there on her own, ready to drop.

'Irene? It's Marc,' he said. He imagined her smiling, that serene smile of hers. Of course she'd know it was him from caller ID.

'Hi. Everything all right?'

'Yes, fine. I had a problem with the delivery, though. I sent the mannequin back. It was manky.'

'Manky?'

'Yes, manky.'

'Is that a word?' she asked, a smile in her voice.

'Of course it is,' he said.

'OK. Call Garb's and have them send out another one, OK?'

'I will. Just wanted to let you know. How are you? Any twinges?'

'No. They're kicking, though. Kicking like mad.'

'My offer still stands, you know...'

'I'm happy here.'

'I could come and stay there...'

'No, Marc. Sweety. I need this. You know?'

'I know, love. I know. But if you need me...David would understand. He's a big boy. He can even manage washing on his own. Cooking, not so much, but you know...he'll manage.'

Thinking of David, Marc twirled his wedding ring, an unconscious gesture that Irene knew well, like someone still getting used to wearing a ring.

She laughed, her laugh calm and kind just like her.

'David would be a bit put out I think, if I stole his husband.'

'You know he'd understand.'

'I know. I know.'

'OK. If you change your mind...'

'Thank you.'

'Bye. Call me if you need anything.'

'Thanks. Really, I don't know what I'd do without you,' she said, and Marc could sense her welling up, which wasn't like Irene at all. Probably hormones, he thought. He didn't know a damn thing about a woman's hormones. Didn't *want* to. There were plenty of things he could live without ever knowing.

'Speak to you later,' she said, and hung up.

Marc put down the phone and after replacing the note to call a supplier, walked back into the shop. He couldn't really do anything about Irene's stubborn insistence on having her babies her way. He understood, but it worried him, especially as she was so far away from everyone.

He sighed.

'Nothing you can do about it,' he told himself.

He heard the bell tinkle again, and thinking he had a customer he rushed back, straightening his hair and then slowing.

The mannequin was right there, the stinking dirty thing, right in the middle of the beautiful dresses, white and cream and ivory, perfection, and a greenish old mannequin.

'You arsehole,' he said, but the delivery driver was long gone.

The funny thing was, it didn't smell the same anymore.

It looked like the delivery driver had traipsed something in, too, because there were dirty footprints leading back to the mannequin.

It took a while to place the smell. Marc thought it smelled like something dead had come in.

*

The mannequin had no legs, no arms. It was a dress maker's mannequin, but obviously an antique, the material aside. People just didn't make mannequins like it anymore. Everything was plastic or wooden, but mass produced with cheap materials.

This mannequin looked like it had been made with love, and talent, a long time ago.

It was little more than a bust, resting on a single long metal leg that looked like iron and that started under a half cut of a bottom and ended in a heavy rusted pedestal of iron, too.

Marc touched the material. Good heavy material, but old and rotten in places. It needed replacing.

It stank, too, but not as bad now he'd opened the door to the shop to let the stink out. Probably, it was just the material and whatever the driver had brought in on his shoes.

Marc cleaned the floor and thought about the old mannequin sitting right there on the shop floor, stinking, making the place look ugly.

But perhaps...if he could take the material off...

It felt like good solid wood underneath...

Maybe, he thought, Irene could use it after all.

*

The weather could be harsh out on the point, but the night was still when Irene headed down the stairs at two in the morning. It seemed like her boys kicked the hell out of her whenever she was in danger of getting a good night's rest, or if they weren't kicking they were sleeping right on her bladder.

She used the toilet on the second floor of her three-storey house, then made her way into the kitchen on bare feet, cold, but refreshing on the bare wooden floors.

She put on the kettle for a cup of tea and sliced some nearly-fresh bread for toast. While she was waiting for the toast and tea she ate a bowl of cereal.

Always hungry, anything she could eat, she did. The cupboards were stocked with enough food to feed a family of ten. Even though she was only really eating for one, or three, depending on which school of thought you subscribed to, she ate all day. Maybe ten times a day. Cereal, for a snack. Fruit, tins – she wasn't a discerning eater, although since falling pregnant it seemed she couldn't drink coffee anymore. Tea would do, though. Maybe the boys didn't like coffee, maybe it was her body telling her what to eat.

A pizza would be nice, she thought.

In a kind of middle of the night half daze she realised she'd already buttered the toast. She thought about it for a minute and put a single frozen thin-based pizza in the oven. It was a tex-mex pizza, with jalapeños and spiced meat on top. She wasn't sure what kind of meat it was, but now she thought about it her mouth watered. She wasn't a fussy eater. Meat was meat, and right now, spiced meat was just what the doctor ordered.

It seemed her body wanted spice. She wondered for a second about the wisdom of eating spicy food this close to her due date, in the middle of the night. She'd heard two things could set off labour – spicy food and sex. She wouldn't be getting the other, but if she wanted a spicy pizza, she *wanted* it. No sense in fighting it.

She ate the toast, drank her tea and ate the pizza.

Then she went back to bed and had the most terrifying dream of her life.

*

There were no lights on in the house, and only meagre moonlight coming through the windows. The house was heavy with silver and shadows. She had no voile or nets across the windows to spoil the view, and no one around to peer through her windows. Naked, she walked along the third floor landing, her bare feet slapping on the buffed floorboards, slightly turned out because her hips were loosening in preparation for the birth.

She looked down at her feet and could see bars of moonlight washing across them. A cloud passed the moon and suddenly the night was almost pitch black. But her eyes were adjusting now. Then she heard it again and knew why she had woken. Her boys were crying out from the nursery.

She rushed along the hall to their room, running in a heavy kind of waddle that she'd developed now she was in the late stages of pregnancy. She didn't know how she could be so heavy when the boys were out and crying, but there it was. She was due in two weeks, and yet...

And yet her babies were crying.

No. That wasn't right. They weren't crying, like when they were hungry or soiled or tired. They were *screaming*. The cloud passed from the moon and she saw footsteps in the hall, leading to her boys' room.

Something was terribly wrong. She clutched her belly tight, protectively, as she pushed the door to their room open.

There was a man in the room, in the shadows cast by

21

the moonlight.

Her children, her twins, were in their beds. She could see their little arms and legs thrashing, her beautiful boys. Terror leaped at her, bit her like a mad dog and almost pulled her down, but her fear was for her babies and not for herself.

The man wasn't moving. She ran at the man, the man who was reaching out for her boys, but then she realised he didn't have any arms.

Somehow, it was worse.

Terrified, she swung her fist, in a kind of desperate and panicked half-slap. She connected hard enough to bruise her hand, and he teetered, like she'd knocked him off balance.

He rocked one way, then the other, then fell down with a heavy thump.

And the thumping continued. Thump, thump...thump, thump. Something regular, like the beat of a bass drum or some large animal's heart.

But it was just a mannequin. The realisation didn't help. It was dangerous, still, lying on the floor.

It rolled over until it was on its back, and then it rose, wobbling until it righted itself.

'Irene,' the mannequin said, though it had neither head nor face. 'Irene...'

Nothing more, but it didn't need to say more, because the voice was always the voice in her nightmares. The words sent shivers down her spine, cold shivers that made her want to wet herself...she tried to hold it, but she still felt her thighs get warm and wet.

'Irene...' he said one last time. 'I'm coming back. For

22

you,' it said in that voice she recognised all too well.

Franklin Jacobs, the man who always haunted her nightmares.

She jumped awake with a shout and the boys kicked hard. She looked down below the sheet as she felt dampness there. She really was wet.

'Oh, fuck,' she said, because her waters had broken, but those words from the dream echoed in her head, even through her panic as she climbed out of bed.

'I'm coming back,' he said. *'I'm coming back.'*

*

Irene rushed down the dark stairwell as fast as a woman in the early stages of labour could go, cursing spicy food in general and tex-mex pizza in particular. Her terror of Franklin Jacobs, Paul's brother, faded as her excitement at the prospect of seeing her babies grew. The dream fled and all that she could think of was her babies, the babies she'd made with her sweet and loving Paul.

Thinking of Paul hurt, though, so she concentrated on preparing for her birth.

She'd timed the drive to the maternity suite. She'd wanted a home birth, but it wasn't practical, considering the nearest midwife lived an hour and a half away. They couldn't guarantee they'd be there in time to deliver her children.

It was an hour's drive to the maternity suite at the community hospital.

She called in and checked with the midwife on duty, an officious woman who rubbed Irene the wrong way

just with the tone of her voice. The officious woman –
Irene imagined the woman actually turning her nose up
as she spoke – asked her a few questions...had her
water's broken? Had she had a show? How far apart
were the contractions...?

All questions she'd been expecting, but she
didn't need to time her contractions to know the babies
were coming, and with twins on the way, hoping for a
natural birth, she couldn't take any chances.

'Wait until the contractions are a little closer...' said
the midwife in her condescending tone.

'I'll be there in an hour,' said Irene down the phone,
and hung up.

'Right,' she said, her belly cramping now, the cramps
coming faster.

Contractions, you *stupid*...she had to almost double
and she did have to puff and pant as the next came faster
and harder than the last.

She didn't have much time. She'd thought...well, she'd
thought she could do this. Now she wasn't so sure. All of
a sudden living out on the point and driving herself to
the hospital didn't seem so smart at all.

But she didn't have a choice now.

For some reason, despite her fear, and despite the
pain, she realised she was smiling.

 She picked up the phone again, because there was one
more call she had to make and she wasn't letting her
boys out until she was good and ready.

Marc answered after the first ring, like he'd gone to
sleep with the phone in his hand. Maybe he had. The
thought made Irene smile again, despite the pain from

another contraction, this one a little weaker, thankfully.

'The boys are coming,' she said without preamble. 'Meet me there?'

'I'll be there, honey,' he said. 'You OK? You want me to drive down, meet you at the boathouse?'

'No time,' she said truthfully, though she didn't want to worry him anymore than she had to. He worried enough as it was.

'Oh. God. Oh...well...oh shit.'

'Marc, calm down, OK? I'll be fine. Just meet me at the hospital. I'll be there in an hour,' she said.

'Get going. Be careful. Promise?'

'I'll be careful. You, too. Love you, honey,' she said, and heard him smile. She imagined David holding his hand in bed. She felt a pang, wishing Paul could have been beside her to hold her hand and give her comfort, but no amount of wishing was ever going to make it true.

She hung up and finished getting ready. It took longer than she thought, because her contractions were more painful than she'd imagined they'd be.

Dressed, bag in hand, Irene Jacobs, nee Harris, closed the front door behind her – she never bothered to lock it – and walked across her sandy porch to the garage, where her Landrover waited. It started first time.

The car was new, so she wasn't worried about the car not starting, but she had read a hundred books on child delivery, just in case. She'd read accounts online at the library of women delivering their own children. She knew it was dangerous, but she also knew she could do it if she had to. She read everything she could get her hands on. She had a kit in the house, now in the car, if she had to deliver the babies herself.

Self-control came readily to Irene, and in this she wanted to be in control.

But already she was beginning to doubt her plan to have a natural birth. As the contractions hit harder, she wondered if she wouldn't be just as happy with the birth if she had an epidural.

But she'd try, and she wasn't a stranger to pain.

She rubbed her shoulders as a shiver passed through her, thinking of all the times Franklin Jacobs had caused her pain and injury.

'No,' she told herself as she drove out of the garage. She wasn't going to think about that anymore. Not this night. This night should be something of beauty.

Twins. She should have gone into hospital a week ago to be induced, but she wanted a natural birth, and though the midwives and doctors had pressured her, she held out. She'd fought for a home delivery, too – she wanted her boys born on the point – but she hadn't fought too hard. She was brave, perhaps, but she tried not to be foolish with it.

She pulled out onto the sandy coast, the dunes and ridges ever shifting, but the Landrover could handle it. There was no road between the house on the point and the mainland. Just hard, sandy work for the big car. The car was heavy, but the tires were fat.

An evening mist was rolling in, and the tide was high. The spit of land between the point and dry land was narrow at high tide, and on rare occasions the tide came high enough to blot out the run altogether. But tonight, it was fine. She had a boat, too, docked out the back of the house, but she hadn't had to use it to make the run yet.

The Landrover roared as she sped across the sand. The bumps weren't helping, they really weren't, but her contractions were fast, now, long contractions with a short break in between. Her eyes were teary with the pain. And she was still forty-five minutes away when she hit the first road.

Thankfully it was the middle of the night in north Norfolk, and there was hardly any traffic on the roads. She gritted her teeth against the pain and put her foot down as far as she dared.

'Won't be long, now, my boys. Won't be long,' she said. She held her stomach with one hand and steered with the other. 'Won't be long, my boys,' she smiled, then screamed as the next pain came and made her lose focus.

She opened her eyes and screamed again, because Franklin Jacobs was in the car next to her. The skin on his face had slewed off, so that she could see his back teeth through his cheeks...he stank, a deep horrid rank smell. He looked like he'd risen from the grave. He reached for her stomach with a knife in his hand.

'Going to cut those puppies out,' he said and she reached out to push him away, felt the knife in her belly...blinked, and he was gone.

Her hand clutched tight in her panic, then loosed and slipped from the wheel as another contraction hit her life a knife in the stomach. The car bounced into the hard verge that ran along the side of the road, bounced back to the other side, and hit a tree broadside with a squeal of metal and the shattering of glass.

The air bag in the steering wheel deployed with a bang and the stench of gunpowder, but the car had no side air bags.

Irene's head cracked against the window, knocking her out cold.

The car came to rest in the quiet night with only the ticking of the cooling engine to break the still dark.

*

Marc paced the hall outside the maternity ward. David watched him from his seat, his legs crossed and stuck out before him. Whenever Marc passed David pulled his legs in. Legs in. Legs out. Over and over.

'Something's wrong,' said Marc, checking his watch again. 'She should be here by now.'

'She's fine,' said David. 'Stop pacing, for Christ's sake. She's fine.'

'She's not. I knew this would happen. I wish she'd let me...'

'She needs time. Time to heal. This is part of it. Let her be, love. Let her be.'

'Where is she then?'

'On her way,' said David, but although he said the words with all the surety he could raise, he was worried, too, because an hour and a half was half hour too long for the journey in from the point. With good weather – for the coast...there was no reason it should take so long. It wasn't like you could get stuck behind farm traffic in the middle of the night.

But, David told himself, there's nothing wrong.

Nothing wrong. Then he heard sirens in the distance.

Marc looked at David, his face pale.

'Don't be daft,' said David. But the sirens got closer.

A few minutes later a nurse came out and rushed toward the entrance. Another rushed through. Both came back ahead of an ambulance gurney pushed by two paramedics, and Irene was on the gurney.

Even as they rushed past both Marc and David saw the blood on Irene's scalp, but worse, the blood on her thighs.

*

Paramedics transferred Irene to a bed, still unconscious. There was a small Accident and Emergency unit attached to the hospital, but the head injury wasn't as urgent as the babies' imminent arrival. Already Irene was coming around, groggy, moaning. Not fully lucid, but not unconscious.

'It's Irene Jacobs,' said the midwife on call. She seemed calm, even though Irene, who she'd met every two weeks since her first scan, was obviously in serious trouble, and the babies more so.

She clicked her finger in front of Irene's hazy eyes.

'Let's have a look,' she said, and didn't need to look far as she could already see the crown of the first baby pushing against Irene's underwear.

Semi-conscious or not, the babies were coming. The pain and the adrenaline were waking Irene up.

'She needs to go to A and E,' said the student nurse watching the delivery with the matron.

'Yes, but these babies aren't going to wait. Now...*help* me, or leave the room.'

She reached between Irene's legs and felt the head, pulled her underwear down and clear.

Three midwives and a locum doctor rushed into the room as the first midwife, Alice Simms, a veteran of hundreds of births, turned the first child. At the next contraction she shouted at Irene.

'Push! Push!'

She shouted for all she was worth, because already she could feel the delivery was going to be a bad one.

Irene grunted.

'My babies? My babies?' she said, but her words were slurry.

'Fine, honey,' said Alice Simms, even though she was troubled. 'Fine, now...push!'

Irene didn't respond, but her body did. The delivery was running on automatic.

'We should get the anaesthetist. She needs a caesarean!'

'Shut up and help me save this baby,' said Alice to the student nurse without turning around from her work. Another nurse checked the baby's heartbeat within the womb. The locum doctor hovered, doing nothing useful as far as Alice could tell, which was just fine by her. She didn't want him getting in the way, because she could feel this one going wrong. She'd seen enough deliveries to know if she didn't work fast they could lose both babies in the blink of an eye.

When the second twin came out with the umbilical cord of the first wrapped around its head, not breathing, blue, she knew just how bad a delivery it was going to be.

As the second baby died on the respirator, despite the other midwives and the doctor desperately trying to revive him, the first baby gave a hearty cry.

Thankfully Irene Jacobs fell unconscious.

Alice Simms laid the first child on Irene's breast and helped him latch on, even though the poor woman didn't even know what had happened.

'Get her over to A and E,' she said, finally, stepping back.

Alice never understood how women could take such pain, but she'd seen plenty come and go, and lost a child herself. She knew it could be done.

But every tragedy hurt.

*

Marc and David came in the following day.

Every day for five days they sat beside Irene, watching her cry, holding a hand each.

She cried her heart out for her lost baby and all the while her friends were there, holding her, comforting her, watching her fall apart, and then, slowly, pull herself into her hard shell.

Marc told her once that he thought of her like some ancient proud monument when he saw her, like a beautiful sculpture, but carved from stone.

She knew part of that was true. But she knew, too, that the pain chipped away at her.

She had some internal bleeding, but she didn't care

about herself. Sam, her baby, nuzzled at her breast.

He wailed and cried like he missed his brother. Of course he didn't. He'd never remember his brother, never know him. They wouldn't play together, go on dates together, or fight over toys then girls. She'd never get to see the two of them through school, or into college, maybe. Everything she'd imagined in her head for two was now just for one, and that kind of sadness is unbearable. That loss of something or someone that never really was. Maybe, in her head, he would get older as Sam did. Maybe she would see him every day as Sam grew and changed and eventually became a man.

Irene cried her heart out every day.

Stillborn was all she knew, and she'd always put it down to the accident.

And that's all it was, she thought. A stupid accident. Like falling for the wrong brother, losing your husband, driving into a verge because you were too fucking stubborn to see sense. The last moments of the accident were a blur to her. She didn't remember why she'd crashed, but she didn't doubt it had been her fault. When she should have come to be induced, she could have witnessed the birth of her twins and remembered the beauty of it. She would have two babies now nestling and nuzzling against her, making that soft mewling sound that Sam was making now.

But no. Same as always, she'd been too fucking stubborn.

'It's alright, honey,' said Marc as he held her hand. 'It's alright.'

She sobbed all the while, all the while Sam suckled

hungrily and her heart broke down over and over. She cried for her baby, for Paul, and for herself.

'It's not alright,' said David. 'But honey, you've got a beautiful baby boy. Hold onto him. He's precious.'

I will, resolved Irene. *I will*. But still she cried, breaking her heart all over again.

But then Sam seemed to look up at her and grasped her finger, and in an instant something changed.

Five days in hospital, a lifetime out. And a family of two again...

Once, it had been her and Paul, and her world had revolved around him. Now, she had a new focus, a new love.

Her heart broke again, holding Sam's tiny fingers in her hand. He was so small, helpless, but adorable, too.

She couldn't see Paul in him, saw more of her, but he had his father's eyes. Deep and knowing, and even though she'd read that newborn babies couldn't focus, she could swear that he looked up at her with love when he fed. Probably not, but he was her responsibility now, and would be for the rest of her life.

She smiled down at him, and at Marc and David.

'I'm ready,' she said. 'Ready to take him home.'

*

Marc drove her home when she was discharged. She could barely walk, her insides hurt so much. She knew most of the pain was where she was ruptured, but some of it, too, was heartache. Something deeper and different and fresher than when she'd lost Paul.

It would never go away, she knew, just like the pain of losing Paul would never leave her. But this was hers, the fault. She owned it.

Just like Paul was her fault, too.

Could she live with this, like she lived with her guilt over Paul, and the constant sorrow?

She nodded silently to herself as Marc drove. Of course she could. Because now she had a family, and she already knew that she'd never let Sam down. Never make a stupid mistake again.

She'd never let him come to harm.

*

In her arms on the way to the car Marc carried her bags and Sam. Irene carried an urn with the ashes of the child she'd never seen. There had been no funeral. She hadn't wanted that. Hadn't wanted the outpouring of grief. Her dead baby was hers, and hers alone, just as the fault was. She wanted that pain, needed it. She held it inside, right next to her love for the baby she'd never watch grow old.

She named him Jonathan, though she never told anyone and never would.

*

Marc tried to talk to Irene while he drove her home, but while she responded to his questions, her answers were short. She wasn't rude. She smiled to let Marc know she was listening, but really, the baby held all her attention.

34

Sam was in the backseat, in the baby carrier. Irene sat in the back, too, staring at the child.

Sam, she'd called him, for her father. Marc thought it was a good name for the boy. Sometimes people have to grow into a name, but the boy was a Sam from the moment he was born.

'Sam,' she whispered. Maybe she thought Marc couldn't hear her, but he could, and he smiled, too. He knew she would have called him Paul, but it didn't seem right to name one Paul and not the other. Maybe it didn't matter now, maybe it did, but Marc understood. It never would have felt right, and she had to do the best she could by Sam. It'd just be the two of them, growing together in the Blue House, learning.

Healing?

Marc nodded to himself. She was still broken from Paul. She would never be completely whole again. But what could she do but to go on? Sam needed her. She'd be there until he needed her no longer, however long that day was in coming. She wouldn't let him down.

And neither would he, resolved Marc.

The boathouse rose from a mild fog, common on the coast as autumn drew on. His car wouldn't make it across the sands out to the Blue House, so he pulled up.

The boathouse was well weathered, with wooden sidings, about fifteen feet high. Irene's boat was back at the Blue House's dock, but Marc's boat was docked just down a bumpy shingled road that led down to the muddy estuary that ran a mile or so inland from the sea. The water was high enough to set off. He pulled his car into the wide gravel park of the dock and helped Irene get out of the car. She was obviously still in pain.

'Can I do anything?' he asked.

'Carry Sam? Can you manage my bag, too?'

'No problem,' he said, and carried him in the nook of his elbow, the baby carrier swinging as he walked, her bag full of baby things on his shoulder.

She smiled her thanks at him with a dim smile, unlike the usual brightness she showed. He wondered what it was like to have such joy tempered by such sorrow, as he unmoored his small boat.

The three of them headed out to the point, the fog rolling across the bow, the boat cutting through it.

He'd never know the kind of pain Irene suffered, never having children himself. His life was insular. He had David, he had his friends, and he had Irene. He'd lost both his parents, but he knew losing a parent and losing a child was different, somehow.

Irene, on the other hand, seemed to take the things that hurt and turn them into strengths. Small; tiny, almost, she exuded confidence. He knew he loved her, and he'd do anything for her. She was the best friend anyone could ever wish for, and it broke his heart to watch her suffer so.

Even though she'd cried solidly for the last five days, there was plenty yet to come, though he knew he wouldn't catch her in a moment of weakness again. He didn't think of her tears as weakness, but he knew she hated people seeing her upset. She was the rock, the sculpture carved in stone, and that was the role she'd taken on. The role she needed to take.

Maybe it was some kind of reaction to the abuse she'd

experienced before she married Paul. Maybe something to do with the horror of losing him.

Marc wasn't a psychologist. He didn't understand the why of it, but he could see the results of the tragedy she'd survived in her every action.

He smiled and looked over his shoulder at her, riding in the backseat of the boat. She didn't acknowledge him, but that was fine, because she was wrapped up in her love for her child. Some parents, maybe they'd blame someone for a tragic death like that. But not Irene. No blame, except maybe that which she bore herself.

Irene sat up front, staring ahead, like she was hungry for that first sight of the Blue House. She seemed so strong, her back straight, her hair blown wide by the wind, like a figurehead on some proud Viking vessel.

But the pain was always there in her eyes, and the way she rubbed at her shoulders, as though shivers passed through her at old memories. That pain would deepen, Marc knew, and he would have to be there for her, when she was ready. Never before, but when she was ready. He would be, too.

She was proud, and strong, and brave, but somehow she would always be frightened, too.

Looking at her proud back, thinking of the horror of this last week, and her life until she'd reached some kind of tranquillity, acceptance, whatever it was that she used to get through each day.

If he'd been through what she'd suffered, he was sure he'd want to die.

Looking at his beautiful, amazing friend, Marc felt like a fool. His present seemed stupid, now. Nothing like enough, and somehow inappropriate, too. But it was too late to take it back, because it was already there, waiting for her in the Blue House.

*

Marc pushed open the door for Irene with his free hand. A sudden gust snatched the door from his hand and it slammed against the jam. The glass in the door didn't break, but it rattled hard.

Marc winced, but Irene barely noticed. All her attention was on Sam in his carrier on Marc's arm. It was maybe the first time he'd known her not to smile at the sight of Blue House. But that probably wasn't so strange. She'd just lost a baby.

'Sam, we're home,' she said. Marc held the door back against the gusting wind as Irene stepped into the front lobby of the house. The lobby was wide, with a split staircase leading to the second and third floors, and the observation post that sat above all.

In the centre of the lobby was Marc's present.

Irene curled her nose up.

'Shit,' she said.

There was a stench there that hadn't been there before. Marc felt embarrassed, but he didn't know why. He certainly didn't smell...but something did. Something he'd smelled before, like meat gone rotten or...shit. Shit and rot. That covered it.

He remembered the smell, then, from before, back in the shop.

Irene looked up from baby Sam and saw the

mannequin. For a moment she had a disquieting sense that she'd seen it before, but she couldn't place it. The feeling passed as soon as it came, and she had no idea why she would have been afraid of a simple mannequin.

Afraid? Now why would she be afraid of it?

Marc had stripped back the worn and mouldering material to find good solid cherry underneath. He'd sanded it, polished it to a high shine with a ton of beeswax. He'd filed the rust from the iron pedestal and polished it so it gleamed like new.

And he was sure it hadn't smelled when he'd brought it over on the boat.

Irene smiled, tired, but a good smile, nonetheless.

'Marc,' she said, not needing to ask if he'd put it there. Of course he had, because she hardly knew anyone else in the whole world. She kissed him on the cheek.

'Thank you,' she said. 'It's beautiful. Where did you get it?'

'The delivery I told you about? The wrong mannequin? Well, this is it. I spruced it up a little, that's all. It's an antique for sure. I hoped you'd like it...'

'I love it,' she said.

Marc thought maybe she'd make it through. Just maybe.

'I swear, it's not the mannequin that smells...'

Irene laughed. 'I know it's not. The sea...smells out here sometimes. Sam's probably pooed, too,' she said, but Marc thought she didn't sound so sure.

'I better head back before dark,' he said. Hardly anyone was stupid enough to risk the waters out to the point in the dark. The sea was untrustworthy, and even

39

though it didn't run deep, it could be fast.

'Here OK?' he asked. She nodded, and he put Sam's carrier down on the lobby's wooden floor and her bag alongside him.

'Be careful,' she said.

He kissed her and Sam goodbye and took the boat back, wondering about that awful smell.

*

Marc shut the door as he left. Irene waited until she heard the outboard motor on his vessel start up, then fade. She kept her coat on because there was a fine drizzle in the air through the fog, and the sea was choppy and cold.

Dark was maybe an hour off.

She put Jonathan's ashes on a large cabinet by the front door and pulled her coat tighter. It could get up a wind down at the front. Already the wind was blowing away the fog and bringing in the rain.

Sam was bundled up in an all in one suit, and the baby carrier had a hood over the top half. There was a rain cover, too, but she didn't think he'd need it. He'd be a hearty boy. 6lb and a single ounce, which he'd probably already lost since being born. She read that babies could lose anything up to half a pound, sometimes more, in the first week after birth. She wasn't worried about Sam, though. He was strong. His grip on her finger was firm when she stroked his face. He gripped her hard when he was feeding, and he fed well.

Yes, he was hale.

She pushed open what she thought of as her front door, the one that led out onto the beach, facing out to sea.

She walked down, Sam in his carrier, the carrier in the nook of her elbow. Over the dunes, through the rain, until she reached the shore.

The sea was getting rough. Maybe a storm was coming in, but it might amount to little more than a squall. A seal popped its head above the water and then disappeared again. The birds weren't wheeling, but bobbing in the surf. The wind blew fine grains of sand into her face, into her hair.

She laid the baby carrier and Sam beside her in the sand. He was sleeping peacefully, his chubby little face scrunched up.

She sat next to him, not worrying about the wet sand on her shoes and her clothes. Things like that didn't bother her at all.

The sea swelled and the rain grew a little heavier while she sat and stared out at the clouds rising and the dark coming in from the east. She watched the gulls and the terns whirl in the wind, crying, like they were singing a dirge for the last of the day.

For the first time since leaving the hospital, Irene felt at peace.

She put her face in her hands and cried.

*

'Oh, Paul,' she said. She didn't know where to start. How do you tell your husband what you've done? When you've killed his child? All that was left of him.

You don't. You tell it to the sea. Vast, uncaring, and the best listener in all the world. Let the water take her sorrow, out on the tide.

'OK...How do I start this?'

She remembered the first time she'd done this. When she'd bought the old home by the sea. The Blue House.

She remembered telling the sea about Paul. How he'd been beautiful in so many ways, ways beyond number. How he'd kissed her every morning when they woke. Even though their time together had been short, she knew he would have done so had they grown old together.

How he'd made her breakfast every Sunday, tried to talk when he was brushing his teeth, given up smoking for her, even though she smelled it on him whenever he went to the pub and how she never said a thing about it.

Truths and lies, like any fine marriage. It was just a matter of keeping the important truths and the important lies straight in your head.

A short marriage, but one that would last a lifetime for Irene. She had no doubts about that. Paul's death was still fresh, but she knew it wouldn't get easier with time. When people said it did, they didn't know. They never knew.

She never thought she'd be telling her sorrow to the

sea again. This time, doing it again for her son.

*

When Franklin Jacobs proposed to Irene Harris her mother cautioned her to sleep on it, and she did.

Sometimes it seemed she remembered more about Franklin than his brother Paul. It was unfair, and stupid, but she'd had months now to mull what was unfair, and what was stupid.

What was unfair was raising a child on her own. It was unfair that she'd been robbed of the only man she'd ever loved.

Nothing made any sense. It never had.

What she remembered most about Franklin Jacobs was his hands. He hadn't been a big man, nor broad, but his hands had been heavy. And hard.

*

Music played on the stereo. It was something old. Franklin's iPod was on shuffle, and she seemed to remember it was some tune she hated. The Stranglers. For the life of her she couldn't remember the tune that night. She'd never listened to The Stranglers since, and never would. Thank God they'd fallen out of fashion.

Franklin drove her to a pub. The Dog and Duck, it was. She remembered that there was a collection of beer mats tacked to the wainscoting, brass horseshoes hanging down from the bar. They sat by the fire because it had been three weeks before Christmas when they first

43

got together. It was a cold night, she wore a wrap-around top that she thought showed her breasts off – just enough, not too much.

That first date, she didn't know. She had no idea what she was doing. She'd always been a pretty good judge of character, but maybe she'd been blinded. He drove her to the pub in a BMW that was only three years old. He was a good looking man, big, thick hair. She liked tall men, even though she was short.

She guessed she'd been beguiled by him, by the smell of him, a deep hard man smell. He worked for a building company, in the office, but he was confident and strong with gymnasium muscles. A little older than her, but not so much that it was weird.

He hadn't started hitting her until they'd been together for six months, but she should have seen it coming after they'd been together for a few weeks. She should have got out right then, the first time he got angry that she wanted to go out with her girlfriends.

If she didn't see it coming then, she could have stopped it any time in the build up to the hitting, but she was young, and like many abused women, the abuse built slowly, until it became normal and she thought it was her fault and not his.

She should have known, but she was young. So young.

The way he tried to control her, stopping her drinking, eventually being such a pain in the arse about her going out with her friends that she just spent all her time with him. He corralled her like a sheep, and by the time he hit her she already knew who the sheep was, and who the big dog was. The hitting wasn't necessary, but then abusers have to take it higher.

By then she'd met Paul, though, and things became far more complicated, because while she was afraid of Franklin and could see no way out, she was falling in love with Paul. Paul was sweet and tender and kind, but he had a streak in him, a hardness that Irene needed in a man.

And Paul knew Franklin for what he was. They were brothers, after all. Paul saw her bruises, and one way or the other it had to come to a head.

Had she wanted it? Had she led Paul to fight her battle, or just let him?

She didn't know. She'd thought about it long and hard plenty of times and never could get to the bottom of it, even in her head where no one else could see if she was guilty or not.

But the fact of it was that Paul saved her from Franklin, and in a way, things panned out from there. Her and Franklin splitting up, getting married to Paul. Paul's death. It all stemmed from that first fight over her.

Maybe if she'd been a little older...a little wiser...maybe things wouldn't have worked out like they did. But then...she wouldn't have had Paul.

And as time moved on, the abuse got worse...she knew she wanted Paul, and wanted him more than anything else in the world.

*

Paul saw the bruise high on Irene's cheekbone.

45

His face darkened like heavy clouds, like steel cooling. The only time she ever saw him angry was on that day, and it was somehow terrifying...but she was naive, then, too, and it was also somehow flattering.

'Irene,' he said. 'Don't think you have to put up with this. You deserve better,' he said.

He boiled a kettle for her. She was in their family home, waiting for Franklin to return from work. She knew he was making tea to keep himself busy, to give him something to do so he wouldn't have to look at her, show her how angry he was.

She saw that his hands were shaking while he stirred the tea. She wondered what it would be like to have Paul's hands on her instead of Franklin's. Paul's *softer* hands, with narrow fingers and light hair on the back. She wondered what it would be like to run her hands though his hair, blonde, where Franklin's hair was black.

She tried to concentrate on something else, and when he brought her tea she didn't look at him, but stared down at the tea, still swirling from being stirred.

'Irene?' he said, not letting her ignore him, though she wanted to.

'I don't know what you mean,' she said, forcing herself to meet his eyes.

He shook his head. 'Yes, you do. You think Franklin's never done this before? He's my brother, Irene. I know him well enough.'

She put her head down. She couldn't bear to look at that angry face, angry, and yet soft, for her. She knew Paul liked her. She wasn't that naive. She liked him, too.

How much did she like him before the fight?

Plenty, she knew. It wasn't all about how he'd saved her, given her back her dignity.

'You've got to leave him.'

She couldn't tell Paul right then, but Irene was half way past beginning to think one of the reasons she stuck with Franklin was...well, it was Paul.

'I can handle it,' she said.

'No,' he said. 'No, you can't.'

That anger lessened as he talked to her, but somehow that was more frightening, because she saw how he pushed it down and stored it away for later.

That night she went out with Franklin. That was the last time she went out with him.

A week later she found Paul in a pub with his best friend Simon. Paul's nose was broken. His front tooth was missing – he would later get a crown over it – but his face lit up when he saw her, and his smile was radiant.

'Oh, Paul,' she said, putting her hand to his face.

Simon pushed himself up. 'My round,' he said. She smiled at him for being such a sweetheart, and took his seat opposite Paul.

'Thank you,' she said. She didn't have to say what she was grateful for. They both knew. He watched her. She watched him.

She touched his arm before Simon came back, and left her hand there. It didn't feel like an awkward gesture. She just wanted to touch him now she could.

She already knew she wanted more.

'Let me buy you dinner. To say thank you,' she said, because she didn't know how else to go about keeping

Paul in her life. She was sure she didn't want him to go. Franklin didn't matter. It wasn't even an issue. That was over. This was now. She didn't want to fuck this up.

'Irene...it's difficult...it's...I don't know...'

'I don't care if you don't know about dinner. Do you like me, Paul?'

Simon came back and hovered. 'Sorry,' he said, putting down three drinks. 'I think I need the toilet now.'

Paul nodded at Irene. 'I'll call you,' he said. She knew he would, and she knew there would be more afterwards. She knew in that nod, and the way he looked at her. Looked her in the eye, but she knew he wanted her, and not just in the ways that Franklin had used her.

'You don't need the toilet, Simon,' said Irene, pushing herself up and feeling lighter than she had since Paul had stood up for her against his older brother.

'But I love you for saying so,' she told Paul's childhood friend.

She kissed Simon on the cheek, but looked at Paul. Paul smiled. She smiled for the rest of the night, sitting with her girlfriends at the other end of the pub, stealing glances at Paul.

Love, first. Marriage second.

Her life was blessed. Then Franklin killed Paul.

But that was old news. She'd told the sea all that already. But it was somewhere to start, and while it hadn't been easy then, and wouldn't be easy now, you have to start somewhere. With a hard story, or an easy one, there's only one place to start.

*

The rain became heavy enough by the end of her telling to make her worry for the baby. He woke and began crying. He was a quiet baby, on the whole, but when he was hungry or tired or uncomfortable, he had his ways of making it known.

She covered his carrier as best she could and with one last look out to sea and the black clouds gathered there, turned back to the Blue House.

The Blue House seemed to rise from the sea behind it, the sea quieter in the bay. She felt stronger again, able to face the rest of the day after unburdening herself to the sea, and stronger still, as always, at the sight of her beautiful house. Something about the sight of it restored her. Those strong weathered boards, the fresh blue paint, the shingle roof...all of it made her feel whole. Since losing Paul she felt best when she was in the Blue House or down by the sea. Complete, again, though neither could ever be a replacement for Paul or her lost baby.

She wondered how people got over such a loss. People kept telling her things would get easier, but they hadn't yet. Maybe the murder of her husband and the death of her son were still too fresh.

She looked down at Sam wailing as she headed across the wet sand and smiled at him. She had something else to fill her life now, her baby. Her son. Her Sam.

When she opened her front door and went back into her house she was smiling. Her hair, long and blonde, hung down in thick wet strands around her face. The rain ran in her eyes, and she used the sleeve of her coat to wipe them clear so she could see.

With a soft sigh she closed the door behind her and the sound of the rain quieted, though Sam was crying up a storm and she knew even on a still day their house would never be quiet again. Maybe when she was older and Sam was away, the house might be silent. She might sit in front of the fire or by a radiator, reading a novel, or sipping hot chocolate and calmly staring out to sea.

The thought of growing older alone didn't frighten her so much now she knew Sam would be there in her heart, growing all the time.

A gentle knowing smile on her face, she turned toward the living room to feed her baby. On the way through she noticed the mannequin in the lobby. But this time she spotted a note tacked onto the back. Marc had written a note with his present.

She smiled again. It was just like Marc to leave a note, not to be around when he did something nice, a little embarrassed, maybe, by other people's gratitude. She took the note, in a thick handmade envelope of pink paper from where it was taped to the old, beautiful wood, and tore it open.

The paper inside was good quality, too. Just like Marc, she thought with a smile.

She read the note, then read it again.

'I'm coming back,' it said.

And beneath that, 'I haven't forgotten you.'

She dropped it on the floor, her light mood gone and cold chills in its place. And in the Blue House, it was suddenly cold, because someone had been in her home.

*

'Marc,' she said into the phone, after walking around the house, checking every room, paranoid that there was an intruder. It was the first time in the six months she'd lived there that she'd locked the doors and windows, and hated herself for it.

But she was scared.

Terrified? Maybe...certainly not far off it.

'Honey? Are you OK?'

'Marc...did you...did you leave a note with the mannequin?' she asked. She asked because she had to, just to be one hundred percent sure, even though she knew before she asked. She knew as soon as she'd read the note, hadn't she?

'No,' said Marc. Of course it wasn't him. 'Why?'

What should she tell him? What could she say? *I think someone's threatening me? I think someone's been in the house?*

She was basing that on a dream she remembered now...but she wasn't, was she? Because Marc hadn't taped the note to the mannequin. Someone else had done that. And of course the note was threatening. There was only one man who would write such a note, and that was impossible, because he was in prison for killing his brother.

Franklin Jacobs, the psychopath.

There was no way Franklin Jacobs was free. After what he'd done, he'd never be free. Never. Even if somehow he could have broken out, escaped, he didn't even know where she lived. Why would he? She'd severed all ties. No one from her old life, save her mother, knew where she lived.

'Nothing,' she said. 'It's nothing.'

Someone had been in her house. She was sure of it. The note was still there, on the floor where she'd dropped it. She wasn't imagining things. It wasn't a dream.

A mannequin stood in her boy's bedroom, and the two boys screamed, and it rocked and rocked in the moonlight.

Irene realised she was crying. She tried to hide it from Marc with a little laugh.

But there was no one in the house now. The doors were locked tight. It was just her and Sam.

Sam, fed, was in a sling, leaving her arms free while she used her mobile. The signal was patchy, the weather playing havoc with the signal.

'Irene, what's wrong?'

'Nothing. I'm just a little spooked.' She laughed a little, again, covering how afraid she was. 'Just spooked.'

But it wasn't nothing, was it, Honey? A voice spoke inside her, and it sounded a lot like Paul. He still had her back.

'You want me to come out? I can do it. No problem.'

'In the dark?'

'No problem,' Marc said, and she could imagine him nodding, even though he was on the phone. He was an animated talker on the phone. She'd seen him phone enough times while they'd been in the shop together.

52

'I don't need you to come. I just...I wanted to know you were there, I guess. It's nothing, though,' she said.

'Doesn't sound like nothing.'

'Pop out tomorrow, if you can. That'll be soon enough.'

Marc must have heard something in her voice. 'I'm coming out now,' he said in his no nonsense voice.

Irene loved him for it, but she didn't want him there. It didn't make sense, but it was her home, and her first night with Sam. She didn't have to make sense.

And she wouldn't be scared in her own home. She wouldn't. Perhaps...perhaps...

She tried to reason it out.

Realised she couldn't.

'I'd rather you didn't, OK?' she said, stubborn as always, even when she should know better. Even as she said it she knew she was wrong. She should have him there...she should go to him...

But you can't, honey...not in the dark...not in the boat...

No. Of course she couldn't. And she wouldn't let Marc risk it, either, because she was...what? *Spooked*?

'I just...I just want it to be me and Sam,' she told Marc over his protestations, while she wondered if it really would be just her and Sam.

But she wouldn't be scared. She wouldn't.

'You want me, you call. Anytime,' said Marc, knowing he wouldn't get Irene to do something she didn't want to.

'I will. Love you. Love to David, too.'

'Love you,' he said, and Irene snapped her mobile

53

shut.

Then it was just her and Sam, and the night, and the rain running down the windows.

And a sound she couldn't place. Like a...like a heartbeat?

At first she thought it was her own, hammering in her chest, afraid despite not wanting to be, and hating herself for that fear.

But it wasn't her heart beating. It was coming from the mannequin.

*

Normally, Irene liked soft light in the house, rather than the big overhead ones, but she flicked on both big lights in the lobby. The lights started dim, because they were those low energy bulbs, but then they brightened and took away all the shadows but for that the mannequin cast. The letter lay on the floor behind it, just where she'd dropped it.

She concentrated on the sound, and became certain that the *thump thump* sound was coming from the dress maker's bust itself.

Was it a bomb?

Did bombs tick? Did they *beat*?

Her heart ran cold, and indecision rocked her for a moment. Sam was in the lobby with her. She was loath to leave him alone while she was so spooked, even though she was sure there was no one in the house...

But how sure was she? Sure enough that she could leave Sam alone?

He was sleeping...he'd wake if someone tried to take him...wouldn't he?

But if she didn't take him, and it was a bomb...

She toyed with the idea of calling the police, but she wouldn't, not after the way they'd handled Paul's death, after letting Franklin get away with the things he'd done.

She decided it couldn't be a bomb. She was being silly. It was all in her head, just fear brought about by that awful dream, and the memory of it resurfacing. A mannequin rocking in the babies' room...remembering two babies in the room...

She placed her ear against the mannequin, sweat beading on her forehead and under her arms.

Thump...thump...

She closed her eyes, dreading the thing exploding. For a second, even though she knew it was just imagination, she felt her head being ripped from her body, her blood splashed across the room and Sam.

'Stop!' she said to herself.

Then it stopped, too. The thump...thump...

Nothing.

Just her imagination. Just her imagination.

She didn't care if that was all it was. She picked up the mannequin and opened her back door, the one that pointed toward land, and pushed the mannequin out into the rain. It teetered, like it had in her dream, but then it fell to the sand with a wet dull sound (like a heartbeat?) and didn't get up again. She watched it for a few moments, just to make sure.

Nodded. Not a bomb. Not *possessed*. Just a fucking mannequin.

She walked back to the lobby and took the letter up, too, then threw that out into the wind. The rain dragged it down and it sat on her sandy porch, but it was good enough.

She wouldn't be afraid in the Blue House.

'It's *my* home,' she said, and at the sound of her own voice the spell was broken.

*

She checked the house one more time before going to bed. For the first time since moving into the Blue House Irene locked all the doors and windows.

Sam stayed in bed with her, curled almost into a ball between her arm and her side. She knew she wasn't supposed to keep the baby in bed with her, but she couldn't bear to be alone. There was a Moses basket next to the bed, but it looked so cold. So uninviting.

It was pitch black out, heavy cloud covering even the lights from the mainland. The rain pounded and the wind rocked the wooden weatherboards of Blue House. All the while Irene lay looking at the ceiling, listening to the house creak. Wondering who could have written the note. Why they would. If she had an enemy she didn't know about, but there was only one enemy and it couldn't have been him.

It couldn't.

Even so, she rolled over, trying to force herself to sleep, with one hand on a kitchen knife and the other on her baby's belly, gently patting every time he stirred.

All night she imagined that she heard a gentle thump

thump thump of a heartbeat, but it was only Sam, under her hand, and that's all it was.

That's all it was.

*

Irene woke with Sam snuggled tightly up next to her and her free hand on a kitchen knife. It took her a minute to wake properly, before she remembered the night before and the note.

She freed herself from her nightwear and began to feed Sam, refusing to start the day spooked in her own home. The doors were locked and the house was secure, and there was also no way that Franklin was free from prison.

Life might not mean life anymore, but he wouldn't ever be up before the parole board. No way. Not ever. A life term didn't mean life, maybe, but 22 consecutive ones certainly did.

No *way* was he free.

'Morning, beautiful baby,' she told Sam as he nuzzled. He stopped and gurgled a little, then went back to feeding hungrily, his tiny fist scratching at her breast while he took his fill. Rustled around him, her white quilt looked like snow, and he like a seal pup out on the west point.

If you were careful and calm, you could walk among the seals. The pups nuzzled and grunted just like Sam, entirely depended on their mother's milk. She wondered if their mothers felt the same satisfaction she did, feeding her child. She would have bet money they did.

Her mobile rang on her old pine nightstand, once her grandmothers, now hers.

She shook her head and set her daydreams on hold while she checked caller ID. Her mother. She should have known. Who else would call this early?

She sighed. It was way too early for her mother to be calling. Anytime was too early for her mother to call.

'Mum,' she said, her voice short.

'Oh, honey,' she said. 'I just heard from Marc. I'm so sorry.'

'Mum,' said Irene, rocking Sam on her shoulder with her free hand, while he brought up little burps of wind, 'I don't want to talk about it. Not yet. OK?'

The last thing Irene wanted to go over was Jonathan's death, and her guilt. If anyone could push her guilt button, it was her mother. And it was just like her mother to call up to...gloat? Was that the right word? Was her mum really that callous?

Irene didn't think she was far from the mark.

'You want me to come back? I can get the next flight.'

'No, Mum. I just want to be alone. OK?'

There was a pause on the other end of the phone. Irene knew her mum wouldn't like it, but there it was. Irene didn't like her. It had taken years for her to come to the realisation that she didn't like her own mother, but once she'd come to the conclusion there was no denying it.

Irene imagined her mother out there in Spain, pacing in the sun, thinking of some way she could muscle in on the drama.

But Irene wouldn't let her because it wasn't a fucking drama. It wasn't some shitty soap on the BBC, but her life and her son's death, and the simple fact was her mother could fuck off.

She thought all this, but she didn't say any of it, because that was what her mother wanted...more drama. Something to tell the bingo club or whatever it was that she was into. Tell Aunty Michelle, or her friend Doreen, or Elizabeth in the shop, or a bunch of other people that Irene didn't know and didn't care if she never knew.

Only then did she realise her mother hadn't asked after baby Sam, or congratulated her. All she wanted was to be in on the heartache. Then she'd go again, and Irene wouldn't see her for another year.

Which would suit her, ordinarily, but not now. She owned this, these early days with Sam. Her mother wouldn't intrude on that. Irene wouldn't let her.

'What did you name the baby, darling?'

Darling rankled, but she pushed it down.

'Sam,' she said. 'After Dad.'

'Oh, honey, that's so sweet. Dad would have been proud.'

'He's a beautiful baby,' she said, but already she got the impression that now her mother knew she couldn't come that her attention was drifting.

No sense in fighting it. She'd learned that long before she learned her distaste for her own mother.

'Mum, listen, I've got to go. It's...only seven here. I've got to change Sam, get ready...'

'Hmm?'

Irene almost smiled bitterly, but she kept it to herself. She didn't think her mother would sense the sad smile on her face, but Irene wasn't like that. She didn't gloat. It wasn't in her nature. And what would she have to gloat about? That her own mother was shit?

'I've got to go, mum,' she said.

'Hold on, Irene honey. I've got news.'

Just like her mum. Worried about herself. Just waiting to trump her daughter, beat her in whatever pointless competition it was that she had going on in her head.

'Frank died, honey. The police called me, you know. A courtesy call, they called it...anyway, I thought you should know.'

'What?'

Suddenly cold, Irene stood. Sam gave a little grumble of dissent, but then fell quiet.

'Franklin. Franklin died. There was a thing in prison...he was killed. I just...I thought you should know. It's over, finally. Over. You can go back...'

'I don't want to,' she said automatically, her mouth running on its own. Her words needed no thought.

She didn't miss any of her old friends, didn't miss her mother.

She missed her father and Paul, and that was about it.

Then she remembered the note. 'I'm coming back.'

The day felt a little darker.

'I've got to go, Mum,' she said, and hung up before her mother could fuck up her day any further.

'I'm coming back,' the letter said...but who, if not Franklin?

*

After a shower and bathing baby Sam, who gurgled

60

while she washed him, lightening her mood, Irene went downstairs and through to the kitchen to make her breakfast; a bowl of cereal and two muffins. Finding she was ravenous she cooked some eggs, too – scrambled, and had them on toast.

She ate at the kitchen counter with Sam in a rocker on the counter top. She rocked him and shovelled food into her mouth. She wiped morsels of scrambled eggs and toast from the sides of her mouth with a napkin and bunched it up on the counter for her to clean up later.

'Hey, baby,' she said. 'What shall we do today...to...'

She looked at the napkin scrunched on the counter and remembered the letter.

Would she recognise Franklin's handwriting if she saw it again? Would the letter still be there, screwed up in the wet sand?

'You won't know 'til you look,' she said, steeling herself. She left baby Sam in the rocker, but moved him onto the floor, in case he rocked himself right off the counter. He didn't move around much, but she didn't want to take any chances.

She moved out of the kitchen, still in her nightwear, and padded out to the hall. She opened her back door.

The letter was still there, sodden.

The words were turned up, and her eyesight was good. She didn't need to bend down to pick it up. It was Franklin's writing, alright. Now she was level-headed in the morning light she was completely sure of it. It was good that she didn't need to bend down to pick up the note. If she had, she might have fainted, not been able to get back up. Because the mannequin wasn't there.

61

*

She knew where it was.

All she had to do was follow the footsteps. The footsteps of a killer that couldn't be, because he was dead.

And yet she held the note in her hand, written with that murderer's hand.

There were sandy sloppy footprints leading up the right hand staircase, and as she followed them they continued up past the second floor, and the guest bedrooms, to the third floor, where she'd slept sound all night with her baby in her arms and someone that just couldn't be Franklin carried on down the hall.

To the nursery.

Footsteps she hadn't noticed on the way down...because they hadn't been there, then, had they?

'Fuck,' she said, and ran in her bare feet through to the kitchen. Sam was still there, on the floor, still but hale.

She picked him up and put him in a carrier that she fixed around her back and waist. Her stomach was still sore, and wearing Sam on her front tired her quickly, but the soreness woke her up, as did the feel of cold steel in her hand as she took up one of the cook's knives.

She was terrified, but she wouldn't wilt, not in her own home. Blue House was *hers*, and whoever it was that was trying to frighten her wouldn't succeed.

The old wooden risers creaked heavily as she stalked up the stairs, holding her kitchen knife with Sam in a sling on her front. Her hands were free, yet even with the knife in her hand she felt somehow naked.

She didn't bother checking the front and back doors, or the windows on the first floor. She knew she hadn't left any open. She remembered locking them for the first time the night before.

Then how did he get in?

Then, heart pounding, she stood at the top of the landing on the third floor. Panting, like she'd run up the stairs, willing herself to go forward. But she was putting off what she dreaded.

And when she got to the nursery, what she feared was true, even though it couldn't be. The mannequin was there, in the nursery, and she was sure she was in trouble, because the beautiful cherry wood was carved, as though with a heavy blade.

Something heavy, like the police had found in Franklin's secret room in the family house. The heavy blade he'd used to kill.

The room stank, a foetid dark and heavy smell. It seemed to be coming from the mannequin.

And on the mannequin was carved with a single word. SAM.

*

Marc picked up the phone on the third ring.

'Marc, can you come out?' He heard the terror in Irene's voice, something he'd never heard before, but unmistakeable in its urgency.

'Honey? What's wrong?' he said.

'Just...' He could hear her sobbing into the phone and

his first thought was that something had happened to Sam.

'The baby?' he asked, dreading the answer.

'He's fine. Please come.'

'I'm on my way,' he said. 'I'm on the mobile in the car, OK?'

He put down the phone and checked around the shop, remembered to lock the till, locked the door, and drove for the coast.

Driving as fast as he could, checking his rearview mirror every few minutes in case someone who thought they were a race car driver was coming up on him. Then screamed, because there was someone back there.

A man sat up grinning in the back seat, and that man looked just like a cadaver, with waxen rotting skin and eyeballs that were yellow and rheumy. He could have easily been weeks dead, but for that grin. That wasn't a dead man's grin. That was a wicked grin that said a knife waited for you behind those tight teeth, a tongue like a blade, a loaded gun and murder with malice aforethought. He was a man who should be in the ground, but would put you there before he succumbed to death himself.

Marc screamed 'No, No!' from pure fear, and glanced over his shoulder, expecting a knife at his throat...but there was no one there.

His hands slipped on the wheel and the car careened across the road, frightening him afresh.

He got the car back under control. Panted for a while.

'Come on you bloody queen,' he laughed, spooked.

'Damn right I'm spooked,' he told himself, because

the man in the backseat of his Volvo had looked a hell of a lot like a corpse. But that couldn't be, because there was nothing there.

No, not *nothing*, he told himself.

A smell that was recently familiar hung in the car, of death and rot and shit.

He wound down the car window and drove faster still, afraid himself, now.

*

The sea was calm on the journey out, the gulls wheeling in the air, hunting for easy fish. Marc's small boat chugged along through the shallow waves leaving a double trail of white behind the boat like the contrail of the jets he saw high in the sky when the RAF flew practise sorties over the land and sea. Imagining he was a jet, flying to his friend's side, the distance passed quickly.

A sense that something was in the boat with him passed quickly, but he couldn't shake the feeling that something was coming. Some *golem*, some bogeyman, under the sea tracing his progress and following his scent, his wake.

At the thought of a wake he began to think, again, of death.

'Nonsense,' he said, but then thought of Irene's panicked voice, and the smell of death.

For some reason he thought of the mannequin, too, and a woman who'd severed her ties to her past life, leaving no trace...but something was coming. He just didn't know what.

'Nonsense. Bullshit. Nothing to it.'

She's just bereaved, and that's all there is to it.

He nodded, convincing himself to shake away a serious case of the willies. Tried to keep as calm as the sea, but he couldn't fool himself. He was panicking. Something terrible had happened, though he couldn't imagine what. For Irene to sob like that...He knew she was hurting, maybe bad enough for those kind of tears...but there was something different about it, some depth of terror that he couldn't imagine, and never would, because he'd never had children.

*

Marc stepped through the door into the Blue House and Irene stepped into his arms. She sobbed onto his shoulder and he looked around, even more worried now.

It was so out of character for Irene to cry in front of anyone. She was rock, the figurehead, the planet whose gravity pulled others in. And yet she held him like a woman drowning, like a baby, needing comfort.

Ordinarily, the house felt warm and inviting, but there was something wrong, some sense that things were out of kilter that had nothing to do with Irene's distress. A hint of a smell, maybe just a prescience of things to come.

'Come on,' she said. 'You need to see it. Come upstairs.'

'What is it?' he said, holding her at arm's length, but not letting her go. He didn't want to let her go for fear

66

she might crumble. This woman, who was once stone, felt like she could turn to dust any moment.

'You need to see it,' she said, pushing him back, then pointing at the footsteps on the floor.

He frowned. 'Someone's been in your house.'

She didn't nod or give any indication that she'd heard at all, but led him up the stairs, on past the second floor and up toward the third, where her bedroom and the nursery were.

Marc's hand went to his throat when she led him into the nursery.

The two cots were still in there, white bars, both made and ready, though the room felt like it wasn't used. He could imagine Irene wanting to hold onto Sam as long as she could. It was in the way she carried him, took him with her everywhere she went, even to the point of bringing him, asleep, in the carrier, just to come up the stairs.

The mannequin was right there, solid, beautiful. An antique for sure. Mutilated with the word SAM carved deeply into the shiny cherry that he'd polished with so much love and care.

'My God...my God...'

'I know,' she said, seeming to regain some of her calm in response to Marc's shock.

'Who? How?'

'I don't know,' she said. She seemed to be taking strength now Marc was here, but his own response was to feel like he was falling apart. He wasn't a brave man, but he wasn't easily freaked out, either.

But this was something else. Something worrying and

frightening both, because someone had been in here and made this threat against his friend. His best friend, but her son, too. Though he'd never have children, now he understood why she'd been so upset, so urgent, on the phone.

Marc took her shoulder. 'Come on, we need to call the police.'

'No.'

'What?'

'No. I don't want the police involved. Not now. Not ever. And what would they do, Marc? What do they *ever* do?'

'What? Irene...someone's been in your house.'

'I know,' she said. 'And I'll deal with it. But I'm not involving the police.'

'Why not? I don't understand.'

'What will they do? What will they do about this, Marc? You know what they'll do? Nothing. They'll pick up the pieces when I'm dead.'

'Honey, don't talk like that. It's got to be...I don't know...some kind of sick joke.'

'No,' she said, shaking her head. Marc could see her stubborn nature coming back now, back through the shock, and what he saw in its place made him take a step back.

She was bristling, and it was anger. Even though she was a small woman, her anger was immense, something that towered like storm clouds.

'I want it out of here,' she said.

Marc nodded. 'Of course. I'm so sorry. I didn't know. I didn't...'

68

'It's not your fault, but...Marc...I don't know who this could be. I've no idea. None at all.'

'Franklin?' he guessed. He and Irene had talked about Franklin and Paul, possibly more than she'd told anyone in the world, and even then only parcelled out in small chunks. There was as much Marc didn't know as he did. But the abuse she'd suffered before Franklin killed her husband was plain to see. Even before the bastard had ruined her life, he'd broken some part of her, too.

'Franklin died,' she said in a blunt, flat voice.

'He's dead?'

'He died and...I...'

'What?'

'I'm frightened, Marc, because I think if anyone could set this up, would do this...it's him. I think maybe he got someone on the inside to come out and do this.'

'Which means you're in a lot of danger.'

She nodded. 'Maybe. But no police. This is my home.'

'Irene...Irene...this is so dangerous. Whoever did this...they're nuts. Fucking *nuts*,' he said. 'We've got to call the police. If you don't want to, I will. This can't...shit, honey. This can't go on.'

She shook her head. 'Don't you dare. I don't want them involved. I just need your help. I just needed someone to know. In case...'

'Don't talk like that,' he said. 'It's not...it's a threat, but nothing's going to happen. I'm going to stay. We'll sort this out together. Catch them.'

She shook her head again.

'I don't want you to stay. It's too much to ask.'

69

But it wasn't.

'I'm staying, and that's final,' he said, his voice strong and determined, 'I'm going to get home, pack up some things, and I'll be back. OK?'

'No,' she said. And the way she said it, he knew it was final.

No matter how forceful he was, some part of him couldn't help thinking about the smell...that dead, dark smell, and how it smelled just the same in the nursery as it did in his car, in his shop. He knew something was terribly wrong. He just didn't know what.

*

Marc dumped the mannequin in the boat and headed back. The journey seemed to take longer than ever, as the boat thumped into the waves, jouncing him and the mannequin in the front.

Every time the boat hit a wave the mannequin would make this hollow noise, thump, thump, thump.

After a while it began to grate on his nerves. Despite the cold, he took off his jacket and padded the mannequin against the hull of the boat, so that it wouldn't make that noise.

It seemed such an innocuous thing. Just a dress maker's palette, a simple thing for hanging clothes from, a *tabula rasa* to build upon.

It didn't smell. It didn't. He hadn't had even a hint of that stink since getting out of the Blue House. Even though he wouldn't be able to smell anything out here but the sea, he knew it was...dormant? That wasn't quite right, but somehow it seemed to fit.

There was something of a threat about the mannequin, and he didn't know why he hadn't felt it before. Before the carving, back when it had first come into the shop.

But then he had felt it, hadn't he?

The way the delivery man had just brought it back. That mouldering old thing, ugliness in among the beautiful wedding dresses...and that stink that came in with it.

What had he been thinking? Giving it as a present to Irene? This horrible, dangerous thing.

Dangerous. Now why would he think that about the mannequin? It wasn't the mannequin that was dangerous, but whoever it was threatening Irene.

Yes. Someone threatening Irene.

He turned his attention away from the bust rocking in the front of the boat to the sea and his driving, weaving between the boats on the way back in to dock. The spume splashed into his hair and face, his unruly hair plastered to his head after a while. It was a lovely feeling. He loved the sea, felt at peace, and for a time, out there in the thrashing waves, he was happy and could almost forget just how wrong things felt.

He drove back to the shop after mooring his boat, and when he got back the first thing he did was walk around to the back, lugging the heavy thing, all solid wood and iron, to the tip. He heaved it into the large green bin and wiped his hands.

He drove home and worried all through his midday meal with David.

'You know you can't change her. She's a stubborn

one, and the only way with a stubborn one is to let them come to you. That's how I got you, wasn't it?' David grinned.

Marc sighed.

'I should call the police.'

David shook his head. 'You can't make her do anything she doesn't want you to,' he said. 'You should know that by now.'

Marc nodded. 'I know. I know. But...'

'But nothing, love. When she wants you, you go. Until then...until then you're here with me...and the phone.'

But he worried, nonetheless.

*

The house felt cold and empty. Like something was missing. Irene wandered the house and cursed herself for feeling so afraid. It wasn't like her to feel fear. She'd never even been afraid of Franklin, but for some reason, now he was dead, she felt fear, true fear, for perhaps the first time in years.

When they'd been together, before the end and the fight with Paul, she'd felt...she'd felt dead herself. She felt nothing. He'd almost destroyed her utterly. Only with hindsight and the love she'd had with Paul did she realise that. The way he'd controlled her, to the point of making it feel like her fault when he hit her. But somehow, she'd come out of the other side. That which didn't destroy you made you stronger...that was so much bullshit. But out of the other side, you were something else. You weren't made stronger, maybe, but if you were lucky, after you were broken you could forge yourself into something new. Paul had helped, sure, but there was also something in Irene that was tougher than Franklin, a man who'd hit on a small woman like her.

Though she was still young enough to have her life ahead of her, she knew she'd never fall for the wrong guy again. Once was enough. Some women, they went back to abusers, time and time again. Maybe it stemmed from having a terrible upbringing. Maybe they saw their dads hitting their mums. Maybe it was a habitual thing, something to do with having no self respect. Maybe Irene, too, would have gone down that route, but she hadn't, and she was stronger than that.

Yet she realised, after checking the house obsessively over the course of the day, that she still clutched the knife. She'd almost forgotten she had it, like baby Sam, sleeping most of the day against her chest, upright in his sling. He was an easy baby, and sometimes she could almost forget she had him there, just like the knife.

But he reminded her why she was checking the house. She couldn't forget the feeling when she'd opened the door to the nursery. Someone had been in the house. Someone dangerous.

She had no doubt they were dangerous. She'd fooled herself before. She didn't do that anymore. Never again.

Should she have let Marc stay? Should she have relented, let the police come?

She thought about it long and hard, but no. Not the police.

Was she scared? Damn right, she thought. But she wouldn't give in.

73

So she checked the observatory, the winding stairs leading up to the tower. She couldn't see the mainland, because there was a light rain in the air again, though she could tell from the darker shape in the rain that it was there. The nursery, the bathroom, her bedroom, all were clear. There were two rooms on the second floor, one a small study she used for paperwork, mainly, with a computer on an old desk that had once been her father's worktop. It still had saw marks on it from his woodwork, but she couldn't bear to part with it. The other room was a guest bedroom. She'd never needed to do much to it, but dusting.

The first floor, with her living room, with an open fire. A second toilet and the bath. Her kitchen, refitted in a modern style, a utility room, the back door and the front door.

She roamed the house, over and over, thinking about all the points that someone could get in – she locked all the doors and windows on every level. The observatory's windows didn't open.

Feeling as safe as she could, she changed baby Sam and put him down in the nursery to rest.

He fell straight asleep and she put on the baby monitor, then sat in her living room, with the window open, listening to the sea.

*

She woke from a deep sleep to screaming. Something about the cadence of the screams told her it was a baby...Sam...*God no, not Sam...*

But something else, too. Jonathan's voice joined Sam's, and they weren't crying in hunger or terror, even, because what does a baby know of terror? No. They were crying in pain.

Jonathan's dead, honey, said Paul, in her head.

So's Sam, said Franklin. For a second, she thought that voice, too, was in her head. But it wasn't. It was on the monitor.

She ran up the stairs, because her baby was back.

And so was Franklin.

*

The door to the nursery was shut when she got there and she wouldn't have shut it herself. She pushed down the handle, an ancient heavy brass thing. The handle wouldn't budge. It wasn't like it was locked because there was no lock on the door, more like someone on the other side, someone stronger than her, held the door shut.

Still she could hear two children crying, almost in unison, but when their breath hitched the screams overlapped. Their voices were similar, but even though he was a week dead, she could tell Jonathan's from Sam's.

'I'm coming, honey, I'm coming!'

She screamed herself now, in rage and frustration, because no matter how hard she pushed the handle, trying to push it down, it wouldn't shift, not even a centimetre.

'Fuck!'

She turned and ran back a few feet and threw herself

at the door, bounced off, hurting herself and not even making the door rattle. It was an old house, and the doors were good and solid.

She hit it again, and again, tears streaming down her face, not for a second questioning why Jonathan was screaming along with Sam.

'Franklin! Franklin! You bastard! You let them go!'

She heard him laugh. She did. She heard it. She was sure. But then the door clicked open and there was baby Sam, screaming, but not distressed, just soiled. The smell of it was thick in the air.

Jonathan wasn't there. The realisation hit her hard, because she was so sure, so sure she heard him. But he was dead. He was in an urn, in the living room, beside her husband.

She began sobbing and picked up Sam and sobbed with him on her shoulder, rocking him harder than she needed to.

*

Darkness fell and Irene stalked through the house, running things over in her mind. It was almost obsessive, the way she thought about it. Part of her imagined it was some kind of dream, brought on by the fear, the afternoon nap.

Some other part of her, the part that was a mother, not the part that hadn't seen Franklin for what he was, thought that there had been some sense of reality about the episode. She hadn't imagined it. Two babies had screamed. She was sure of it.

Was she just as sure she'd heard Franklin on the baby monitor?

She just didn't know.

What she did know was that she was dog tired, and sore, and just wanted to go to sleep.

She took everything she needed for the night into her room, put a chair under the door. She curled up again with baby Sam, who just wanted to sleep and feed all the time, and fell asleep.

*

Baby Jonathan took her hand, only he wasn't a baby.

She looked down at him, his toddler's hand in hers. He smiled up at her, and even in the midst of the dream, knowing it was a dream, her heart broke because he was a beautiful boy.

Paul's blood, as he would have been.

Could he talk, in the dream? Could *she*? She'd never spoken in a dream before. Her dreams were in pictures only, sometimes, strangely, in smells, but there never was any sound or conversation.

She tried her voice and found it worked just fine.

'Honey, are you Jonathan?'

He nodded, but she saw that around his throat there was a black mark, like a rope burn, running right through the space his windpipe was.

Like he'd been strangled, and in her dream she realised that he was still dead, always would be, but it was enough that his spirit, his ghost, was here now. She didn't question why or how he could be here in her sleep, but he was and that was good enough.

She followed where he led her, down the stairs, through the lobby, and out of her back door.

The sky was dark, like it was the middle of the night. There was a light mist sitting just above the water. The mist wasn't high enough to obscure the lights from the mainland.

Jonathan led her down to the shore. She held back – she knew she shouldn't leave Sam behind – but somehow Jonathan seemed to know this, to read her mind. Of course he could, she reasoned, because this version of her stillborn son was in her mind. He didn't exist. He hadn't been a toddler, never would be.

Jonathan understood, but pulled her down to the sea, then into the sea, but she found she could walk. She stepped onto the mist, not the water, and walked toward the mainland.

It seemed as though the mile to the mainland passed in an instant. There were no boats in the bay, though there should have been hundreds, all moored and bobbing in the high tide, the rusty and forgotten and the new and the proud. Yet the bay was empty but for her and Jonathan walking on that strange mist.

With a thought she was before her shop. She didn't mean to be there, but Jonathan took her where she needed to go.

Her son put his finger to his lips. *Quiet*, he said without words.

Together they passed the front door to Beautiful Brides, and headed down the rear alley, where the waste was stored until the bin men came to take it away.

Shh, he said again with the same gesture. She heard his sounds in his head though his mouth didn't move.

He crouched in the dark, and she crouched beside him, watching.

Something was coming through the dark, and it thumped, bumped. Like a heartbeat. The thing that came through the dark was dead. She understood that, too. It was why Jonathan could see it, and she could see it, too, because Jonathan alone could show her such sights.

The beating became louder as the thing approached, and she saw that it was a man surrounded by black mist, like smoke, but something ethereal and not quite there.

The man was dead. That much was obvious. His skin had slewed from his face, showing the muscle underneath. A rotten man, and she could smell him as he came closer. He was a man, but something else, too. She felt Jonathan trembling beside her, understood that this man must not see them. Darkness and evil came from him, just as strong as the smell of death and rot.

The man, the corpse, looked around, like he was checking for observers. He looked right past them in the darkness, hiding. She shivered as his gaze past over her, and for some reason she thought she should recognise him, though he didn't look familiar and she didn't understand the need to know who he was. It didn't matter. All that mattered was how dangerous this moment hiding in the dark was.

But his gaze didn't stop with them. It turned back to the bins in the back of the shop and then he opened the bin and she saw it. The mannequin. It began to beat. She could see the wood pulsing as the man drew it from the bin. Pulsing exactly like a heart beating, though it wasn't in a chest. It was just a dress maker's mannequin, and yet it was more.

The man hefted the mannequin in his arms and walked straight past them toward the light at the front of the shop.

Jonathan tugged her hand and pulled her after him. Even in the depths of the dream she was terrified of the man. She shook her head, but Jonathan was in charge of this dream, this powerful toddler, this spirit of her flesh.

He tugged and she couldn't resist. She followed him and he led her to the front door of the shop, where the corpse was picking the lock.

She was even more afraid, because now she knew that the locks on her house were inadequate. She understood perfectly that this thing had been in her house. Locks were no bar to it.

It opened the door and walked in. She heard the lock snick closed again.

Jonathan looked at her sadly. He pulled her down and touched the side of her head.

Remember, he was saying. *Remember.*

*

Irene's mobile rang her awake again in the morning. She panicked, remembering the word SAM carved...the threat...

The man in the dream. A dead man in a dream that could pick locks.

But it had only been a dream...just a dream. Nothing

had changed. She'd slept like a log and woke to the phone, not in the middle of the night with a psycho, a phantom, leaning over her.

Baby Sam nestled in the crook of her arm again, a replay of the day before. She took a moment to look at him. A beautiful baby, already putting on weight after losing it during the first week. His face had lost that kind of squished look that newborns have, and in sleep his face was smooth and beautiful.

She checked caller ID on her mobile and groaned.

'Mum,' she said.

'Morning, honey.'

Irene checked the time. Five AM. Her mother had no concept of time, and that other people had lives.

'Mum, it's five in the morning here...'

'Oh, I'm sorry.'

'What is it?' said Irene, not wanting to get into a slanging match with her mother first thing in the morning.

She called her mother Mum, but always thought of her as her mother. Somehow, the distinction between the words in her mouth and head kept her mother distant. She'd been hurt by her too many times over the years to let her any closer.

'I heard what happened to Franklin,' she said.

Irene could imagine her mother, almost gleeful, wanting to impart her piece of gossip, to be involved in some kind of drama.

Irene didn't need it at any time of the day, least of all five in the morning.

But it wasn't worth it. Maybe she could put the phone

down...go make a cup of tea...come back and say 'uh-huh' a few times. She wasn't really needed for a conversation with her mother.

'Go ahead,' she said, nestling the phone between her ear and her shoulder. She extricated herself from Sam, sound asleep, and piled pillows around him so he couldn't fall out of bed.

The floors were cold on her bare feet, but they woke her up all the way.

'He killed himself,' said her mother with triumph in her voice.

'Good,' said Irene. She didn't know what she felt, but it was good. Definitely good.

Her mother was still talking, but Irene suddenly found her legs wouldn't hold her and she sank back to the bed. Shock? Relief? She didn't know. Dizzy, for sure.

'They never found his heart,' her mother said, and the world rushed back in with a thump. Thump. Thump...and she remembered her dream, totally, fully, from holding her young son's hand, to the corpse behind the shop...to the mannequin.

*

'Mum, what? What did you say?'

'They never found his heart...'

'No. All of it,' said Irene, her voice shaking now the reality of the news hit her.

'Well,' said her mother, with barely disguised glee, 'He made a, what do call it?'

Irene suppressed her impatience. Her mother would

get to it in her own time.

'I don't know what 'it' is.'

'A deal, kind of thing, but about dying, you know?'

'A pact?'

'That's it.'

Get to the point, she thought, her heart cold. She'd wished the bastard dead so long, and now she found herself panicking...still early...a Saturday...Marc wouldn't be going to the shop just yet...

It was still early, and this time she *would* call the police.

But she had to know.

'Well, it's pretty sick.'

Did she really need to hear? Did she have time?

She decided she did. She felt this was important.

'His cell mate cut him up.'

'Stabbed him?'

'No. Cut him up. Like, in pieces. Cut out his organs and ate them.'

*

Paul Jacobs knew there was something wrong with his older brother from as early as 10 years old. Maybe before, but he didn't really remember. Kind of like some abused children forget, willingly, or because their minds can't take it at that age. People have different ways of coping. Some talk. Some forget.

Paul forgot for a time.

*

He'd found Franklin with the cat back when he was too young to understand, but with the second cat after that kind of cusp of childhood that comes around 10 or 11 years old, just when children are thinking about beginning a new school. Maybe a child hits some kind of peak, some brain spurt, around those years.

But when he found Franklin with the second cat he remembered the first, and the first had been the worst, because back then Franklin didn't know what he was doing. The second time around, he didn't make nearly as much mess.

*

Franklin was hunched over something at the back end of the garden, where their dad put the garden rubbish, the cut grass, the trimmings.

Franklin was sixteen and Paul was eleven years old. He looked up to his older brother. He loved him unconditionally, and when he went out into the garden he was merely interested to see what was so fascinating down there in the shadow of the white birches, three of them, that grew low down. Between two of the birches there was a pole which they used like a monkey bar, shimming across from one tree to the other. At least they used to, until Frank seemed to lose interest in playing with his little brother.

Paul found porn in his brother's bedroom one day. He flicked through the pictures, kind of confused. He didn't really get it, but he knew it was something secret. He put them back, just as he found them, because even then he knew some secrets were for the keeping.

But there was something about the set of Franklin's shoulders that said he was concentrating hard, and maybe this was the kind of secret they could share, and Paul was ever curious.

'What you doing, Frank?' he said, walking toward him, where the three trees hid them from the house and the neighbours.

'Come and see, dippy,' said Frank.

Paul didn't mind being called dippy, because he'd always loved his brother.

'Is that...is that...'

'*Is that...is that...* Yes, dippy. It is.'

'What are you doing?'

Paul hadn't seen the spike through the cat's stomach at that point, but when he got closer he saw what Franklin had done.

'Shit, Frank! Shit! Mr. George is going to kill you! Shit, what have you done to Bess? Shit. Frank. Frank...'

Paul remembered later. Not all of it.

He remembered Frank. Remembered the fevered look on his brother's face. A look like he got when he came out of his room in the afternoons, when their father was out at work sometimes and he was supposed to be watching Paul. But Paul thought those magazines might have something to do with that feverish look in his face.

Frightened, Paul turned to go, to tell their dad, back in the house.

'Touch it,' said Frank.

'What? No! I'm not touching it.'

'You afraid?'

'I'm not afraid. It's gross. It's...it's wrong.'

Frank shook his head. 'Dippy, you're such a pussy. It's just a fucking cat.'

In some ways, the swear was more shocking that the cat. Looking back Paul understood that his brother had pushed him, pulled him, everything shy of forcing him to touch the cat. But it had been the same. The same.

'I don't *want* to, Frank. Don't make me.'

'I'm not going to make you, but you're going to do it anyway, because it's cool.'

'I'm not.'

'Look,' said Frank, and twisted his fingers inside the cat. The cat yowled, and it's back legs kicked out. 'Touch it here and you can make it dance.'

'I don't want to,' said Paul, crying. The cat didn't have a look he'd expected. It seemed to him that the cat looked sad.

'Do it or I'll tell dad what you did.'

'What? I didn't do anything!'

'I'll show him Bess. Tell him it was you. You're just a kid. He'll believe me.'

'You wouldn't. I'll tell.'

'Touch him or we'll find out.'

And to his shame, Paul did it. He cried, and he was sick afterwards. He touched the cat inside and watched the cat's back legs dance while it screamed in pain and threw up all over the cat.

'I'm telling,' he said. It didn't matter. It was wrong and he was wrong. He knew, even at eleven years old, that what he'd done was so wrong. The worst thing he'd ever done. He could feel sweat on him, the taste of sick in his mouth, and the cat...

The cat was dead.

*

'Shit,' said Paul, his tears thick and fast and his bile rising again.

Frank was on him fast, too fast for Paul, still just a child, not even a teenager, to run. Frank was holding the little paring knife their mother used to peel the potatoes, but that knife was sharp. He held it up under Paul's throat.

'If you tell anyone. Anyone. Not just mum and dad, but anyone at all. I'll find out and I'll fuck you up like Bess. Got it?'

Paul couldn't nod, couldn't swallow.

'Uh,' he said.

The whole time he couldn't take his eyes of the cat, tailless, with a spike from his dad's shed through its belly.

That was the second time.

Frank got better with practise.

When Paul finally confronted his brother, trying to save Irene from him, he threatened him.

'Leave her alone, Frank,' he said. 'I'll tell everyone what you did back then. I'll fucking tell everyone,' he said.

Franklin laughed. 'Little brother, you think that's the worst I've ever done?'

*

Marc took a call on his mobile that he never expected. It was Saturday morning and he was on the way to Beautiful Brides to open for the day.

'Is that Marc? Marc Jones?' said a woman he didn't recognise.

'Yes, who's this?'

'You don't know me, but I'm Irene's aunt. Her mum said...she said if there was an emergency, I was to get in touch with you. I tried your home number...I got your...partner? I didn't know if I should call you, too...'

Irene had fallen off the map, as far as everyone but her mother was concerned. Marc was the first point of contact outside of Irene that her mother had, in emergencies.

Marc slowed to a stop in a passing spot on the narrow road.

'What's happened?'

'I can't get in touch with Irene. I've tried, but I don't know if I have the right number. I tried last night but I couldn't get through. I don't know...'

'It's alright,' said Marc. 'Calm down and tell me what's wrong. Is it Maureen?'

'She died last week,' she said.

Oh, shit, thought Marc. Poor Irene. He didn't know Maureen, and his first thought was that he was being selfish, maybe, not to spare a thought for Maureen, but first and foremost he was worried about Irene and how she would take it.

On top of her stalker, the mysterious man that was

threatening her, this was just too much. He pulled on his hair and put his head down so his forehead was hovering over the steering wheel.

The woman, he'd forgotten her name already, was still talking, but nothing was sinking in.

'I'll call you back, OK? I need to go to see Irene, let her know. I've got your number now,' he said.

'OK. I'm Sally,' she said.

Of course he hadn't noted her name, because she hadn't told him before. He was shaken, though. Shaken badly. He just didn't have the first idea of how to break the news to Irene after so much loss.

'Thank you, Sally. I'll talk to Irene.'

Poor, poor Irene.

He hung up and swung the car around in the tight spot and headed for the boathouse instead of the shop, in a cold sweat, his stomach churning.

*

Sam began crying while Irene's mother was on the phone.

'Hold on, Mum.'

She picked up Sam and began feeding him. Some women had trouble breast feeding, but she'd taken to it straight away, and Sam was latching on just fine. She felt that instant of release, that let down, as he began guzzling, making satisfied noises in the back of his throat.

'OK, Mum,' she said, watching Sam feeding and feeling urgency build in her, even though she now knew there was no way her...what? Stalker? No way he could be Frank...and yet...who else would it be? It didn't make sense, but it felt right.

'So,' said her mother. 'He got his cellmate to cut out his organs. Are you sure about this?'

But Frank had been dead right from the start, thought Irene. And she remembered her dream, Jonathan leading her by the hand to show her the corpse, the dead man, breaking into the shop.

Urgency, dogging her, but she knew she had to hear it. It was still early, but she needed to get off the phone. Call Marc.

'I need to hear it,' she said, though all of a sudden she wasn't so sure she did, and still torn two ways.

'He cut out his liver, his heart, his kidneys. Ate his eyes. Cut out his heart.'

Irene felt bile in her throat.

'Jesus,'

'More like the devil,' her mother said, and laughed, which seems cold and callous, somehow, even for her.

'Yes...what happened to his cellmate?'

'Got transferred to a psych ward. No one to cut him up. You see, he wanted to join Franklin in the afterlife, but Franklin would never have let him join. He was a queer. He fucking hated him. Wasn't really a death pact, either.'

'Mum?'

Her mother laughed again. Mid-laugh something changed and she knew she wasn't speaking to her mother anymore.

'I'm unbound now,' said a man's voice she knew so

well, one that sometimes haunted her dreams.

'What? Mum...' she said, still clinging to the illusion, not even beginning to think what it meant. Chills raced up her spine, starting at the base and right into her head so she couldn't think anymore.

Because it just couldn't be. None of it could be real.

'Your mummy's dead, honey. Dead and done. I'm free. *Free*. Do you fucking understand? I'm coming for you, Irene. I haven't forgotten. You took my brother. Now I'm going to take everything away from you. Everything. That queer, David? He'll be dead before this call is over.'

She didn't know how, or why, or what was going on, but she screamed into the phone. 'Fuck you! Fuck you!'

She hung up, slamming her phone shut.

The phone rang again, straight away, and she threw it across the room, smashing it, making baby Sam scream.

Then she roared in frustration, because she had no way to get to David and Marc, and because that fucking monster was in the shop.

She picked up Sam and rocked him on the way down the stairs. She picked up her keys and forgot she had no car, just the boat.

'Fuck!' she shouted again, the word echoing around the lobby.

'Come on, Sam,' she said. 'There's a phone at the dock.'

She pulled on her coat, quickly, desperately frightened now, and opened the door to take her boat across the bay, but she didn't have to, because Marc was right there, and he was crying.

91

*

'Jesus, Marc. I'm so glad to see you,' she said and threw herself into his arms.

'I'm sorry, honey,' he began, and she just knew it was terrible news. The phone call replayed in her mind. The dream. The monstrous man, the dead man...Franklin back to life.

'David's dead, isn't he?'

'No. Why would you think that? Honey, I'm so sorry,' he said, 'It's your mother.'

Irene sobbed, just once.

But she knew, didn't she? She knew, when her voice changed and she was speaking to Franklin. Of course she was dead.

Yes. She knew that too, now. She couldn't deny it any longer. She didn't understand it, but she knew the truth of it.

Franklin was back and there was no doubt in her mind that he'd done it...done what he'd been trying to do all along. Done all the things the police had said at the trial, all the things they'd never known, things she'd never known. Things he did to Paul's body after he'd killed him.

'I know. She's dead. Marc...'

'I'm so sorry, Irene. I'm so sorry.'

'Marc, shut up,' she said, because she felt how short time was. 'David's in danger.'

And she knew where the danger was, too. Not just Franklin, but some power held in the mannequin. It

92

didn't make sense, she didn't know how she knew, but she knew well enough not to doubt it.

Jonathan's spirit had shown her. The dream had been true. All of it, right down to the fact that her baby would have been a handsome toddler, and good looking boy, and a fine man.

Franklin coming back, the mannequin...somehow the two were connected. Like the mannequin was a focus for him?

No. Something...something else. But it was important. It had all started with that cursed thing.

'Marc, you've got to know...I spoke to mum a few minutes ago...'

'That's impossible,' said Marc, shaking his head. 'Honey, she died last week.'

'What? Last week?'

'I'm sorry,' said Marc again. He didn't know what else to say.

'I know it wasn't her,' she nodded. 'I knew it wasn't her. It was him. Frank.'

'Frank's dead, too, though.'

'Frank's back. Don't ask me how. Don't. I don't know, OK? But Marc, what did you do with that mannequin?'

'I threw it out the back...'

'The mannequin, Marc...it's dangerous. I'll explain on the way...'

Marc shook his head. 'Irene, I don't understand.'

'Doesn't matter,' she said. 'Trust me, OK?'

They climbed into the boat, baby Sam wrapped up warm and up against her in his sling, so she could smell his hair even in the sea breeze.

Marc drove from the back. Fast as he could, trying his mobile on the way...but nothing. Nothing at all.

*

David pushed the key into the front door to Beautiful Brides and opened it wide. Something subtle he couldn't put his finger on told him Marc was in the shop...a smell...a hint of body warmth, something.

A second later he held his nose, because it wasn't body odour, it was decay.

'Marc?' he called, but his husband didn't answer. It wasn't like Marc. Even if he'd been on the phone, waving his hands around like he always did, he would have said something. Put his hand over the receiver, shouted out.

'Hi, love...honey...' all the names people in love call each other, and sometimes the names they call each other when they're pissed off, too.

'Marc? I need to speak to you...' but nothing. David checked the small staff toilet, kitchenette, at the back of the shop, and the tiny office. Marc wasn't in.

Call Irene, he thought, pulling his mobile out.

He turned to go outside, to get a signal, and realised there was someone there.

A man stood between him and the doorway. He had his arm around a mannequin, an old scarred wooden thing that he'd seen Marc working on. He didn't know where the man had come from because the little bell above the door hadn't rung.

There was something wrong with the man, the way he

was standing.

And the mannequin...there was something wrong with it, too. And that smell.

David, fear rising, tried to make his throat work, form words. But his mouth was suddenly dry, because he sensed death in the room. He was a stranger to death, but now he was here...there was no mistaking it.

The mannequin, too. It wasn't scarred when Marc worked on it. Now there was something scratched into its chest.

'Hello,' he said to the man. 'I'm sorry,' he said, his voice cracking as he spoke, 'but the owner's out for a minute.'

'I'm unbound now,' the man said.

A funny, jarring note hit David. Like when you see or hear someone insane out and about on the town. Like that, but worse, because the man...the man smelled of death.

He could read what the mannequin said now.

SAM

He turned and screamed. Some shambling wreck of a man walked toward him, a patchwork corpse. A flap of his face was hanging down, and his lip had rotted and fallen off. He wore a name tag, and David, even in his terror, could read that the man was a doctor.

'David,' growled the monster, and as David tried to run the man behind hit with something hard and he went out.

*

95

Marc parked his small car in the narrow street where the house he and David nestled between the other houses. All were painted bright colours. It was a good street, never any trouble, though sometimes people coming out from the pubs in the centre of town took to pissing in the little alleyways that led to the small back gardens.

'Wait here,' he said to Irene.

'No way,' she said, unbuckling her seatbelt. She held Sam. Against the law, and dangerous, but in the rush to reach the mainland and David she hadn't thought to bring the carrier.

She pushed open the door and was out of the car before Marc.

'Come on,' she said. 'Come on.'

Marc walked fast to the front door and pushed the key in. As soon as the door was open he knew Marc wasn't there. But in the way that he had to double check a door was off, or the hob was off, if someone asked him, even if he knew he'd done it, he had to double check, because Irene shouted out 'David!'

'You check downstairs,' he said, taking the stairs up two at a time. No sound of the shower, no sign of David being in. Usually he would have music on, or the television. Marc was more of a reader, but the noise never bothered him, same way as people who live together get used to using the bathroom at the same time, or a small kitchen. They just revolved around each other.

'He's not down here,' Irene said.

'Not up here, either.'

'The shop?'

Marc nodded. 'I don't know...maybe he's looking for

me. I didn't have time to tell him. I wanted to get to you...'

'I know. Come on, let's go.'

'No, honey,' he said. 'We're here now. It's too dangerous. You've no carrier.'

'No, I'm coming.'

'No you're not,' said Marc. He hardly ever denied Irene anything. She was his friend, but she was his partner in the shop, too. He'd never go against her, because of the friendship, but in this he was unshakeable.

'I'm going. You're staying here.'

'You don't understand,' she said. 'I told you, but you're not getting it. He knows where you live. He knows where I live.'

'You're safer here than in the car,' he said, remembering why she'd lost Sam's twin in the first place. He couldn't risk it, and he wouldn't let her.

'Lock the door,' he told her. 'I'll be back.'

'You can't...'

'There's some other explanation, Irene. There's got to be.'

He locked the door. Stood outside for a moment with his eyes closed, thinking things through. It couldn't be that a dead man had come back to life. Part of him thought that maybe this was some kind of trauma, coming out in Irene. But then he remembered the word carved into the mannequin.

'No,' he told himself as he slid into the driver's seat of his car. 'No.'

She wasn't insane. She wasn't having some kind of

illusions because of grief.

David was in danger, and he had to trust in his friend, like he always had, and always would.

He pulled out into the light traffic and swung the car toward the shop, and hopefully, David. Unharmed.

*

David came around in the tiny office of the shop and cried out in terror again, but he didn't pass out. God, he wished he could, because the crazy fucking monster was looming over him, grinning, and up close he stank, stank like the rotted corpse he was.

The man's face was falling off. Rot had taken him. The eyes were rheumy and yellow, and a maggot crawled out from his cheek. Flies buzzed around the room, then returned to the man's neck, where the fed on his putrefying flesh.

'I ate Franklin, you know,' said the man.

Terror and bile rose in David's throat. He felt sick from the stench and the fear both.

'Please...whatever you want...I...'

'You'll do anything?' said the man.

David tried to get up, but he was bound tight in the office chair. He pulled with all his strength, but he wasn't a strong man and the bonds were secure.

'See, David, husband of Marc, friend of Irene...I'm going to take *all* of you. You know who I am?'

'Please...no...I won't...I won't tell anyone,' said David, but thinking, *he's dead, he's dead.*

'I'm Franklin, you fucking stupid queer, and I'm death

walking. And no, you won't tell anyone.'

Whatever he did, he knew he was going to die. He thought of Marc, leaving him behind. He thought of the pain.

'Please...'

But that was the last coherent thing he got to say, because by then the dead man opened up his shirt.

The flesh underneath had already begun to putrefy.

'I ate Franklin's cellmate, you see. He ate Franklin. A little bit of him lives on in me.'

Then he started cutting.

But not David.

On himself.

'You ever hear of a canopic jar?' he asked, but David couldn't ask. For some reason as the man began to pull out his liver, still standing, the only thing David could think of was the taste. The awful taste of rotten flesh as it was forced past his lips, then his mind broke utterly.

'I practised on my brother, you know,' he said, but David wasn't listening anymore.

*

The corpse fell to the floor. David smiled and swallowed the last morsel. At first, it had been a struggle to get this one to feed, but after a while things went easier.

By the end, David wasn't David anymore.

*

The little bell over the front door tinged as Marc pushed

the door open. It reeked in the shop. Reeked like that first day, that God awful stench of death, rot, shit...every vile thing he could imagine.

'David?' called Marc, his voice urgent, his heart pounding. Someone was in the shop. He could hear shuffling, someone coming from the back of the shop. He didn't know what to do. He picked up a tiara from a display and held it before him.

'I've got a weapon!' he shouted, but then felt like a tit because David emerged from the back of the shop, licking his lips like he'd just polished off a snack.

'Marc? I wondered where you'd got to. What the hell are you planning on doing with that?'

Marc grinned, relieved.

'Oh, thank God, thank God. Oh, babe...'

'Whatever's wrong?' said David, frowning.

'Thought you were dead,' said Marc.

'What?'

'Irene got a call...her mother died...Franklin...' Marc shrugged. 'It's a long story. We think...well...oh. Oh shit...the mannequin...'

'Where's Irene? Where's Sam?'

'At ours. We went there first, but...oh, David. God, I'm so relieved you're OK.'

'I'm fine,' he said, shaking his head. 'Tell me everything. Get me up to speed. Is Irene going to stay with us?'

'No. We're going there. Out to Blue House.'

Marc kissed David.

'Jesus, you need to brush your teeth. What the hell have you been eating?' he asked.

David just smiled as Marc locked the door behind them.

He checked out the back, but it was refuse day, and the mannequin was gone. He breathed a sigh.

David and Marc got into the car, thankfully away and on the way to get Irene.

But Marc couldn't shake that stink from his nose. He smelled it all the way to their house, like a ghost that was haunting him.

*

The mannequin stood in the back office of Beautiful Brides. The body of one Dr. Ingmar lay on the floor beside it. His stomach was cut open, his organs missing. They would never be found. His eyes were missing, but he was already a long time dead.

The mannequin seemed to be making a sound, like a soft thump, like a heartbeat, but not for a second would anyone mistake the sound for Dr. Ingmar's heart, because that, too, was gone.

Dr. Ingmar, who worked at the psychiatric unit, had seen better days. Even on the way to Spain he'd been decomposing. In reality, though he'd been walking and talking for a week, he'd been a corpse since being forced to eat Franklin's cellmate.

PART TWO
THE BLUE HOUSE

'Little brother, you think that's the worst I've ever done?'

Paul took a step back, his fists still clenched.

'What are you talking about?'

Franklin laughed. 'Let's just say I've had a bit more practise since we were kids. Let's just say that, eh?'

'Ah, Frank. Frank, what have you done?'

'You don't want to know, do you, Paul? Do you?'

Paul thought, no, I don't. I really don't. Because he was about to beat his brother senseless, if he could, and he didn't need to know anymore than that. After this night, win or lose, he was done with Frank.

'It doesn't matter, because I love Irene,' said Paul. 'You leave her alone, and we're done here.'

'Leave her alone? You fucking idiot. I haven't even *started*.'

Paul nodded. Put his head down. Took a breath and swung.

*

Paul stepped into a straight left that smashed his lip and broke his front tooth in half.

His first instinct was to swing again, because he was mad and angry and full of some kind of confused love for his brother that bordered on hate. Maybe even went over the border.

But he didn't. He stepped back, and Frank's wild

swing went past his head. He felt the air as Frank's fist passed his cheek. Then, maybe because he was cold, things seemed to slow for a second.

That second was all he needed. His next punch connected with Frank's ear, a hard right that rocked his brother and made him stumble. Paul followed in with a left uppercut that broke Franklin's nose, then a miss that caught the back of Franklin's head as he went down to the pavement outside their house.

Frank began to rise and Paul knew he couldn't let him get back up. It wasn't the kind of fight where you shook hands after. Wasn't the kind of fight where the loser held up a hand, said they'd had enough, or they were done.

It wasn't a fucking match, and Paul knew it right from the start.

He swung his right foot as hard as he could into Frank's ribs, figuring if he killed his own brother at least Irene would be safe.

You think that's the worst I've ever done?

Frank's ribs shattered with the first kick. The second knocked him out cold and broke his jaw.

The police didn't get involved. Maybe if they had, Paul would have lived. So would a whole lot of other people, too.

*

Irene jumped as the outboard motor gave a cough and died. For a second she panicked, thinking of the loud thump thump thump she'd heard, thinking the mannequin was a bomb, or something. She'd dozed in the boat despite it being a cold day, colder up here on the coast.

'We're here,' said Marc from the back of the boat. The boat coasted the last few feet into the boathouse, under cover and out of the biting wind.

Irene looked down at Sam, in the carrier on her front. He was sleeping soundly, as he usually did. His cheeks were ruddy from the wind but he didn't seem fazed by the cold or the sharp breeze blowing across the bay.

'Thank you,' she told Marc, and gave David a smile, too. 'Thanks, both of you, for this. I don't want to be alone for a while.'

'It's fine,' said Marc, mooring the boat next to Irene's and lending a hand to Irene to step off onto the wooden plank.

'It's not fine,' she said. 'I feel bad, dragging the two of you out here.'

'Wouldn't have it any other way, honey,' said David. 'I'll get the bags. Get the baby out of the cold. I'll be along.'

Irene nodded and as her feet hit the sand her legs almost gave way.

Relief, she thought. Relief to be home. She opened the boathouse door and there it was, like it was rising from the sea itself.

The Blue House.

*

The first thing she did was feed Sam. Marc put the kettle on for tea, flicked on the gas grill because Irene hadn't eaten all day and she was feeding for two, or so he figured. He sliced almost a whole loaf of fresh bread, a little past its best but good enough for toast.

When he came back in Irene had her feet up on her red couch, with Sam atop her. Both were sound asleep.

He heard the front door snick and padded on socked feet through to the lobby. David shivered and dumped the bags beside the door.

'I've never been here before,' he said. 'Where's the guest room? Or are we on the couch?'

'No,' smiled Marc, remembering that David didn't like the sea. In the rush he hadn't thought of it. He loved his husband afresh right then, because despite his fear he hadn't complained once, and all for Irene.

'There are guest rooms on the second floor. Irene and Sam are sound asleep. You want some toast?'

'Sure,' said David. 'I'm starving. I'll follow my nose when I come back down.'

'Kitchen's not too hard to find,' he smiled, and turned back to his toast before it could burn.

*

David put the bags in the guest room on the west side of the house, facing the point. He placed them on the bed, and stood for a while, staring out to sea. He made no attempt to unpack, but licked his lips and tried to remember the taste of flesh.

He unpacked the important things. He'd brought some little extras along for the ride. David and Marc weren't psychopaths, so they hadn't had everything he wanted when he'd been packing, but he had enough. There was a meat tenderiser, a good cleaver, and a sharp knife that would get through flesh.

He could feel himself beginning to decay already, so far from the focus of his power. But he didn't think he'd need this body for long.

Things would end this night, and he'd have what he came for.

What he'd wanted all along.

His own flesh and blood. A vessel that could hold him. Sam.

*

Marc and David ate a simple lunch of buttered toast at the old kitchen table while Irene slept with baby Sam on her chest.

'She must be exhausted.'

'She's had so much stress...so much loss. I'm not surprised,' said Marc.

'I guess not,' said David. 'Is there anything we can do, do you think?'

'I don't know. She's pretty independent. What do you think?'

'Make sure all the doors and windows are locked tonight. We don't want him getting in.'

'Irene said he can pick locks, this man. This...fuck...I don't know if I really believe it. A guy coming back from the dead.'

'What do you think it is?'

'I don't know. I'm worried she's losing it.'

'What about the mannequin? Sam?'

'I know. It's weird. I can't explain it.'

'Well,' said David. 'I think the best we can do is be here for her, look after her. Make things a little easier. She's just lost her son, her mother. That's got to be so tough on her.'

'Yeah.'

'Tonight, well...sounds stupid...'

'What?'

'How about we take it in turns?' Keep watch. Like security guards,' said David, laughing a little, because the thought of the two of them acting like security guards was kind of funny.

Marc could see the funny side, too.

'Sure. You take first watch? I'm better early than you.'

'Done,' said David, taking a last bite of his toast and feeling a tooth shift in the gum. He smiled and turned his head to one side.

'Got a bit of toast stuck,' he said, and pushed his finger into his mouth. He pushed the tooth out of the gum. It came out easily. He swallowed it.

'There,' he said.

They both smiled. 'Maybe meet up for a little rendezvous, say, around three?' David winked.

Marc laughed. 'Trust you to get horny at a time like this.'

'Should I go away and come back again?' asked Irene from the doorway with a smile.

Marc flushed.

'No need. Just talking shop,' he said.

'Right,' said Irene and helped herself to some toast.

*

Irene put the stereo on then sat at the kitchen table while the boys went through the house, checking every window a second time.

She didn't know if she could let them take a watch all night, but she knew for sure she'd sleep better with some company in the house. She made tins of soup for their supper, with the last of the bread toasted, dripping in butter.

Irene always thought of butter as part of a sandwich, or toast, rather than just something to spread. She heaped the butter on and as they ate it swirled on top of the soup.

'David's taking first shift,' said Marc. 'No arguments,' he said.

'I don't know.'

'No arguments.'

'What would I do without you two?' she said. Honestly, she didn't know. She looked at her two best friends, watching her intently. Both had only come into her life since she'd moved out to the coast and bought the shop, hiring Marc, but within a month they'd both become a part of her life.

She'd known them now for longer than her marriage had lasted.

'Boys, I love you, you know that, right?'

David smiled. 'Honey, you're talking like something terrible's going to happen. Nothing bad can happen while I'm on duty. Me big. Me strong.'

She laughed, although even to her it felt a little strained.

'You want to listen to some music, play cards, something?'

'You look like you want to get to bed, and I swear, that baby does nothing but sleep and feed.'

'They do at this age. He'll be up and around soon enough, after uncle Marc and David's finest china.'

'Can't wait,' said Marc, 'But you go to bed, if you want. We'll watch the fort.'

David nodded and smiled, too. She noticed he had a tooth missing. She was going to bring it up, but she was so god damn tired and she knew David was vain about such things.

David farted.

'David,' said Marc.

'Sorry,' he said with a grin. 'Pea and ham soup,' he shrugged.

'Jesus,' said Irene. 'That's my cue.'

'Night, boys,' she said, kissing them both. 'Love you.'

She took Sam in his carrier, wriggling his little chubby fingers, upstairs.

'Uncle David's stinky, isn't he, baby?' she said. Baby Sam giggled, she thought, but it was probably just wind.

*

Darkness fell. Marc watched it coming in, like something rising from out of the sea. There was no sun, the clouds were heavy. Blackness just came from the horizon, out of the east, until the Blue House was swamped in it.

'Do you think he's coming?' he said to David.

'The man?'

'Yes.'

David shrugged. 'With other people here? Doesn't seem his style. Seems like a sneaky kind of fucker.'

Marc frowned. It wasn't like David to use bad language. He'd been farting, sniffing, now swearing like a fish wife...maybe in his head he was getting into character, the dragon slayer, the protector of the damsel.

Didn't work for him, but they'd been married a long enough time that he wouldn't gainsay him. If David needed to man up to feel braver...

He knew well enough that he didn't feel brave at all.

'Maybe...maybe we should be armed, or something.'

David shrugged again. 'We could get a knife, something...I don't know. I mean, if it's some kind of stalker and that's all it is...then we accidentally kill him...we could go to jail.'

'I wasn't thinking of killing anyone...just scaring him off.'

'Might work...'

'I'll get a knife.'

'Get me one. A *big* one. If it's for scaring, a big one would be best, you think?'

Marc nodded. 'I guess that makes sense.'

Marc wandered into the kitchen and rifled through the drawers.

He turned round and David was in the doorway.

'Got a couple of knives,' he said.

David smiled. 'Here, I'll take the big one,' he winked.

Marc shook his head. 'Boys and their rulers,' he said, but he smiled, too.

*

The evening passed slowly, David waiting impatiently for Marc to go to bed.

He could feel the change coming over him, burning his insides. He tried to keep the wind in, as his stomach, his intestines, his blood, turned rotten. He was decomposing and this far from the focus of his reanimation, the mannequin, there was nothing he could do about it. The decomposition slowed though it couldn't be stopped when he kept the mannequin close.

Now he was falling apart.

'Let's turn the lights low,' he said, trying for darkness to hide the change coming over him. If Marc screamed, if he made a fuss...

Then Irene might wake. The baby might wake. She might run, and keep on running, and he only had one chance at keeping alive for longer, so he didn't have to keep doing this, putting himself into a vessel that just couldn't hold him.

He needed Sam, and he was falling to pieces. Literally. He'd already swallowed down three teeth, and he could feel others coming loose.

His skin was starting to loosen, too. It wouldn't be long before Marc noticed. Already he was looking at him with some kind of worry in his eyes. That worry would soon turn to suspicion, then screaming, then everything would be fucked. It was hard enough trying to be his husband, his lover. It would be harder still to silence him without killing him before the screaming began.

*

'I'm going to bed,' said Marc, and David, a straight man in a gay man's body, could have kissed him, or more likely stabbed the stupid fucking queer through the eye.

But that wouldn't work. Stab a man through the eye and he'd scream his fucking head off...unless you got through to the brain, but even then it was no sure thing. Go for someone's eye and it's a natural reflex to turn the head. Most times, trying to take an eye out, the best you got was a glancing blow.

The only sure way to get a clean, silent, death – not something that usually bothered Franklin – was to make sure your victim was incapacitated first.

'You OK to take first watch?' asked Marc, yawning.

'Still perky, Sarge,' said David with a tight smile, trying to hide the fact that his front tooth had just dropped onto the carpet before he could swallow it.

'Kiss?'

'Haven't brushed my teeth, honey,' said David. 'Kisses in the morning.'

'OK. Wake me up when you're tired,' said Marc.

David blew him a kiss and settled in for the wait. He would have to hold it in, hold in that murderous rage, until Marc began snoring. It wouldn't be long. He knew Marc was a heavy sleeper, because he inhabited not just David's body, but David's mind, too.

That was why the change had never worked, back in

the early days, in the Black Room. Because of the eyes. The eyes were where the mind resided, truly the window to the soul. Inhabiting a dead shell never did work – he'd never managed to transmute a soul until he fed a man the eyes of a black man he'd killed.

Fuck, but he got a shock when that blue eyed man opened his brown eyes and screamed.

But Franklin had learned since then.

He'd learned plenty.

*

Marc lay down on the bed, worrying about David, who didn't seem right. He lay there for a long time, looking up at the ceiling, worrying about David, about Irene, about the man Franklin, who was coming back, as Irene said. Coming back.

He turned in bed. The bed, iron, had old fashioned springs below that squeaked and squealed every time he turned. He must be making enough noise to wake the dead. He worried about waking Irene and Sam, sleeping upstairs. Maybe Irene, too, was tossing and turning just as he was.

He turned his mind back to Franklin. Could the dead come back to life? Of course they couldn't, he thought. But that was the problem, wasn't it? Because Irene didn't have any enemies.

It had to be someone that Franklin had befriended in prison.

But it didn't feel right.

He remembered that dead, rotten smell.

Like someone had crawled out of the grave, and no matter how hard his intellect fought it, he *felt* it was true. Franklin was coming back.

Coming back as *what?*

He didn't know. He didn't care. He felt the blade of the kitchen knife in his hand, somehow frightening yet with a comforting simplicity.

He turned on his side again and put it under his pillow, though, because he didn't want to scratch his face in the night and end up taking his eye out or cutting off his ear.

He thought about the mannequin, and its place in all this. He thought about that awful smell, and then thought for a moment how much like that smell David's farts, all night, had been.

He worried about that for a while, too, but then he fell asleep, on his back, and began snoring.

*

The house was dark as David listened to Marc turning and the bed squealing for what seemed like forever, but then the noise of the bed ceased and Marc's heavy snoring came from upstairs. He itched to go straight to Irene and Sam, to take what he really wanted, what he needed, but there was no way this fucking body would last.

He needed Marc, first, and Irene and Sam second. Once he'd killed Irene, Sam would be his for the taking.

His own blood, at last. His last chance at a body he could take, he could live in. He'd have to teach Sam, let him learn, let him mature enough to live a life...but he

115

could do that in the Black Room.

He could bring him up, make him strong...and when the time was right, whatever vessel he was in at the time, he would cut himself open and feed himself to his nephew.

He smiled a grim smile as he stalked up the stairs, the rot moving fast, now, maybe too fast.

With his canopic jar – his mannequin – he could make a vessel last for weeks on end. Without it, his rot accelerated until it was dangerous for him. Dangerous, because if the decay was too fast, he would become a putrefied mess on the floor, his muscles and tendons beyond use. He would waste away, unable to move, unable to kill and take a new body.

Every moment longer that he stayed this far from the mannequin was perilous.

His body, already rotten on the inside, felt the urgency.

That urgency translated into swift footsteps up the stairs. Urgent, but trying to be quiet, he stalked along the landing on the second floor, on the outside of the floor boards, near the wall, where the floorboards were less likely to creak. He stood outside the door, watching the man on the bed, fully clothed, staring up at the ceiling, sleeping with his eyes closed.

Time would be short, and Franklin knew he'd have to move quickly now. He knelt, his leg popping as the ligaments in his knee gave way. He didn't feel the pain, because really, this body was dead already.

He took out his tools from under the bed. The tape, the rope.

He slapped the tape over Marc's mouth and Marc tried

to sit up, but David, *Franklin*, smashed a fist into Marc's solar plexus and the fight went out of him immediately.

Something popped in Franklin's elbow with the force of the punch, but still he smiled his gap-toothed smile, because it wouldn't be much longer now.

Not much longer at all.

'Try to make another noise and I'll leave you here while I cut up Irene,' he said, and wound the tape around Marc's hands. Once he was in Marc it would be simple enough to sit up and cut off the bindings.

Marc's eyes were wide with terror, and shock, and then, yes, understanding.

Then David, or Franklin, knocked Marc out cold with a fierce, well-aimed punch to the temple.

Then took the knife he'd brought to his own flesh. He dragged the knife down, performing a classic Y-incision on his own torso.

He felt no pain. But as he cracked his sternum with the meat tenderiser he had brought with him, he was worried about the noise.

Rushing now, he pulled himself apart, pulled off the tape over Marc's mouth, and began to feed his unconscious husband the essence of himself.

He held his hand over Marc's nose while he fed bite sized morsels into the unconscious man's mouth. The reflex to swallow or choke was natural.

Of course, he left his eyes until last, and in the end, it turned out nice and easy.

*

Irene moaned in her sleep while Marc became Franklin. For a second, on the cusp of waking, she thought she heard something, but she didn't want to stir, because it was a beautiful dream. She didn't want to let go. Instead of reaching out at the sound, something she found frightening even through the veil of sleep, she pulled herself further down under, into the sweet dream...the dream where her boy was still alive.

*

Jonathan took his mother's hand again.

He was still a toddler, but for some reason, in this dream, she didn't question it. She didn't feel the need to question it. It was what it was, and it was a good dream. It was sweet and her heart leapt at the sight of her beautiful boy, as he would have been.

He had unruly hair, a blonde thatch, like hers, not like Paul's.

He pulled her up from her bed and with a hard face that didn't fit his cute features, he drew her onward, out through her door (she didn't need to move the chair from underneath the door handle, because this was a dream) and down the stairs. She followed, smiling down at the back of his head. He didn't look at her any more, but pulled her down, urgency in his walk, like a little boy eager to show his mother something exciting, like a new secret place.

He took her downstairs and showed her such sights.

She couldn't see anything but David, leaning over Marc on the bed. Marc thrashed for a second, then he was still.

For a moment, just a fleeting thought, Irene thought she had stumbled upon Marc and David in an intimate act. But then she saw the truth of it.

David's body fell to the floor and she could see that his chest was cracked open, his insides were gone. He was a hollowed out, grotesque shell.

She didn't know much about physiology of people, when it came to the insides of a person, but she understood well enough that parts were missing.

And his eye sockets were a bloodied raw mess.

Marc sat up on the bed and for a second she didn't see Marc, she saw Franklin. She remembered the Black Room, as the papers had called it, and knew now what it was that Franklin had been doing...

And had, somehow, succeeded.

It should be impossible, but there was no doubt. In the dream Irene understood fully that David and Marc were gone. Franklin had used them up.

Her best friends.

She could cry, but you can't cry in a dream. You can watch, you can run, you can cry for help, but no tears come in dreams.

Marc, but *not* Marc, took a knife from David's dead hand and cut out his husband's eyes. He looked at them, in his palm, smiling, licking his lips, like he was about to eat them.

He turned his face up and seemed to be pointing at Jonathan.

'You want them, kid?'

She felt Jonathan's nod, some tremor running through

her hand, and Jonathan reached out and took the eyes.

'No!' she shouted, 'No!' but it was too late. Her boy was eating the eyes, then he turned to her and his face, too, was Franklin's.

'It'll come to pass,' said Marc, no longer Franklin. Jonathan, with Franklin's features, nodded too.

'It'll come to pass,' he agreed, through a mouthful of eyeball. 'If you don't wake...'

Irene couldn't cry for her dead friends and her lost son. She could scream, and she did. She didn't want to dream anymore, not this dream. She wanted to wake, wanted to wake, wanted to wake...

*

She woke with a scream and knew he was coming. She heard his footsteps, heavy and fast, on the wooden floors.

She didn't waste time doubting her dream. Her knights weren't coming.

Franklin. No doubt in her mind. Marc and David were dead, but she couldn't even think about that, because now everything was about Sam. She understood what he wanted him for, instinctively, and because it was obvious.

Franklin, in anyone's body, could have killed Sam anytime he wanted. He didn't want Sam dead.

He wanted him alive.

A sob escaped her throat and she held out her arm, knife in hand. Her hand shook. The door burst open and Franklin was in the room.

He had a knife of his own. Only it wasn't a knife.
It was a cleaver.

*

'Is that it? All the fucking effort I've put in, and all you could come up with is that shitty knife?'

'Fuck you, Franklin.'

'So you know?'

'I'll kill you.'

'I'm already dead,' he laughed.

'I'll keep killing you 'til it sticks, then,' she said with more force than she felt. Her bladder had already let go. She felt weak, impossibly weak. Her knees shook and her hand shook.

But this was the man that had terrorised her, killed her husband. Wanted her son.

The hand that held the knife became steady. Her teeth cracked as she bit down. No more talking.

'You can't win, bitch,' he said. 'I killed your two queer boy buddies. This body'll last a little longer.'

'Because of the mannequin.'

'My little canopic jar, if you will.'

She didn't care. She didn't know what that was, but she could guess. Some piece of him was inside the mannequin. She remembered the thump thump thump she'd heard.

'Your heart?'

'Bingo, bitch. Bingo.'

'I'll burn it.'

He laughed again.

'Finished?'

She shook her head. 'You're not taking him.'

'Let me show you something,' he said. He put his hand, his left, against the door jamb. Swung with the cleaver and the tips of two of his fingers tumbled to the floor.

He grinned at her and showed her the stumps. There was hardly any blood. Because the heart in Marc's body wasn't beating. Marc was dead, and Franklin was just riding him.

'You understand you can't hurt me,' he said.

She sobbed, again, but then gritted her teeth against the terror and frustration, because now she understood that she really couldn't do anything against him.

He would take her son. Make him...him.

There was no way past him. No way she could beat him with the little knife she had, especially when she couldn't hurt him. He was already dead.

She threw the knife at him instead. Threw it as hard as she could and wished her aim to be true.

*

The knife stuck in his shoulder. He didn't bother to take it out. Just laughed.

'I practised this, Irene, honeybunch. I *practised*. I'm dead, but all I've got to do is take another body. Can't take yours...men don't fit into women. Don't kid yourself. I know you want me inside you again. Tied up. Remember that? Man, you came so hard when I put my hands around your neck. But I don't think I'm up to the task now, eh?'

'Fuck you. Just fuck off.' She ground her teeth against tears of despair, but what could she do?

Kill yourself?

She didn't like that voice.

Kill Sam?

She liked that voice even less, because that sounded like the old her. The one that had let Franklin degrade her, make her hate herself until Paul made her whole again.

Terror rose up in her but she weighed it down with anger, let the sea take it.

Let the sea take it, said a different voice, and this one sounded like Paul.

She liked that voice, but she didn't understand.

She turned her head, because it wasn't Paul's voice. It was...

Jonathan was floating outside her window.

He held his hand out for her. Trust me, he seemed to be saying. Trust me.

She understood what he wanted her to do. Understood, even though the words weren't there. Kind of like telepathy, on a basic, childish level. Just images.

She understood.

There was no other way.

She looked at Sam on the bed. His face puckered, ready for a scream. Like he knew what she had to do.

She stood at the foot of the bed. Maybe eight feet between her and Franklin. Franklin grinned.

He knew she couldn't win. He'd take pleasure in cutting her up.

She turned and looked one last time at the window. Jonathan still floated there, holding out his hand.

Franklin couldn't see her other son, Sam's twin.

She could. For a second she closed her eyes, steeling herself for the pain. Hoping against hope that Jonathan's spirit was real enough not to lead her to her death.

She had nothing but blind faith to go on.

But she had more, didn't she? She had the love of her dead son, in whom a part of Paul's spirit lived on, too.

Before she could let her fear overrule her, she ran to Jonathan and gave her life over to him, let him take her, as she flew smashing through the window and out, three floors down with glass falling all around her.

PART THREE
THE BLACK ROOM

Paul hung in the Black Room, thinking, *you think that's the worst I've ever done?*

The Black Room was thick with dried blood, piss, shit, maybe some kind of fluid from stomachs, like bile or acid. Pieces of people. That was difficult to think about.

Think of Irene, he told himself. But thinking, too, that he wasn't going to get out of this alive.

Don't kid yourself, Paul. You know you're not getting out alive.

He knew because after looking around the room a hundred times while he'd been captive, his eyes kept returning to the man hanging from a hook opposite him. The man was drugged. A bag hung from a pole with a drip feeding him something which kept him sedated or alive. Paul wasn't sure which. There was only one back. He figured it couldn't be both.

Maybe the pain and despair kept the man sedated. Maybe he was in some kind of coma.

The man hung by hooks through his flesh, holding him upright, though his head sagged against his chest. Paul thought the man was going to suffocate under the weight of his own head if he didn't get help soon. And he wasn't going to get help. Help wasn't coming. He knew that just as well as he knew he was dead himself.

Paul didn't know how long the man had hung from those hooks, but the blood was crusted, and below him there was an old pool of urine and some faeces mingled in with the blood.

The only indication he lived was the gentle rising of his chest and the snuffling sound that accompanied each breath, almost like a snore, but more laboured.

Other people hung from the ceiling, too. Parts of people, husks, people in various states of mutilation.

Two women's bodies hung down, hooks through what remained of their flesh, where it had not been flayed from their muscles. One of the women's hands had been removed. Perhaps, Paul thought, she had fought back. Perhaps it was just another part of Franklin's psychosis. Maybe he had some aversion to her fingernail polish. Maybe she smelled of cats.

Once, Franklin had practised on cats.

Now, he was practising on people.

Practising for what, Paul didn't know.

But you're about to find out.

When Paul first woke he thought maybe the sight would drive him crazy, but it had been two days now, dozing, waking, seeing the dead and mutilated and the poor man hanging from the hooks.

He wasn't going crazy.

He was past that, right the way through it, into some kind of hypersanity. He remembered everything that ever happened to him, remembered feelings, smells. Even just the memory of the things he'd smelled in his life was strong enough to obscure the rankness of the room, this black room with old blood splashed across the walls, the floor, the ceiling.

'Hey,' he said again. His voice cracked as he said it, dry. He tried to work some moisture into his mouth.

'Hey!'

The man continued to hang, unresponsive. If anything, his breathing became even more laboured.

Paul wanted to throw something at the man, but he couldn't, because he too hung from hooks in the ceiling that pierced deep into his flesh, and the only movement he could manage was a gentle sway that ignited pure agony in every part of him.

Those hooks held him fast while he waited for Franklin's return.

*

Irene looked up at the dawning sky; dull oranges and bright blues and deep purples fading off to the west. It didn't make sense to her. When she'd died, throwing herself through a window, it had been night.

The moon was still in the sky, low. A crescent moon, but ethereal in the light of the rising sun. It would have been a warm and clear autumn's day if she wasn't dead.

Jonathan leaned over her, his hand on her face, and she knew she was dead because she could feel him like she could in dreams. Sam was gone and she was dead and the afterlife fucking hurt.

But being dead wouldn't hurt, would it? Would it?

Her back hurt, her legs, her arms. God, her head hurt so badly she couldn't move.

'I'm paralysed?' she asked Jonathan. The toddler shook his head.

'No,' he said, short and sharp, like a child just learning to talk, 'no' being one of his first words. He pronounced it more like 'naoh'.

He understood her perfectly. A child of his age, just able to say no, wouldn't know what death was. This Jonathan, this dream child, understood far more than his apparent age, even if he could only speak the speech of a toddler.

But, then, Irene reasoned, if she wasn't dead, she was paralysed, surely. She tried to lift her hand, but couldn't move it.

A hot, burning thought passed through her head. *Sam was gone.* She pushed it down, somewhere under the surface of her thoughts, where she could cope with it.

She knew Sam wasn't dead. But she also understood the horrors in store for him. She'd identified Paul's corpse. She knew full well what Franklin was capable of. She knew what he planned.

She couldn't move, but she could cry.

She cried and her head would not move. Her tears ran down her face, along the hollow of her temples, and into her hair. She could feel the tears. She could feel the pain of losing Paul, and the memory of what Franklin had done to him. The fresh pain, still, of killing her baby that she would have named Jonathan, and pain like a knife in her insides, knowing that Franklin, dead Franklin, now had her one surviving baby. Marc and David, too – gone. Her only family in the whole world was Sam. Her only reason for living.

'I can't move,' she told Jonathan. Her tears ran on. She cried in despair.

But if she was paralysed, why did she hurt so fucking much?

'No,' he said. *'Naoh'*

'He's got Sam.'

Jonathan nodded, a sad look on his face.

'Can you help me?' she said.

Her son pursed his lips in what was a surprisingly adult expression. He nodded again, like he could say no, but not yes, though he understood the concept and all her words.

He didn't try to help her up, but kissed her on the cheek. Then he thrust his clumsy, still babyish hands through her flesh and into her neck. Those baby fingers passed through her flesh like something solid, though her son was nothing more than her imagination, maybe a ghost, but as fragile as smoke. The pain she could have wished away, but then her son would be gone and she wanted him here. The agony she felt might get her living son back.

She bore the pain and the breathlessness while he felt around within her neck. Then, with an audible crack, louder for Irene as it travelled up through her bones into her head, her neck returned to its correct place. It felt as though he'd just pushed her vertebrae into the correct place.

She slammed her teeth shut against the scream that wanted to come out when she felt that crack and the ability to move once again. Her limbs jerked, once, as the bundle of nerves in her slipped disk settled.

The pain she thought she'd felt awoke afresh. Agony. Pure hell. Everything hurt so badly. She wriggled her toes, her fingers, and found that she could move just fine, though God, it hurt to do so.

It didn't matter how much she hurt. She had to get moving.

It was daylight already.

Maybe she was afraid he would come back.

But then Jonathan thrust his hand into her chest and squeezed and this time she did scream, because she felt her heart kick and beginning beating with that thump thump that she'd come to loath, and she understood why Franklin hadn't cut her up, why he'd left her where she was.

He'd left her because she'd been dead.

Jonathan nodded, as if to confirm it, though she hadn't said anything aloud. She didn't need to speak to him. He was dead and he felt her.

Irene bit down against the pain as she tested out an arm, a leg, and found that nothing had been broken. She wondered if she'd somehow slipped a disk in her neck when she fell, cut off the circulation to her brain. There was no point in trying to figure out how she'd died. She was back, and Sam was waiting.

Could she do it? Could she get up, now Jonathan had given her the gift of life, even though she'd robbed him of his through her stupidity?

She raised both arms. There was blood on her right arm. Sand was in the wound, yellow grits deep inside her flesh. It would fester if it wasn't cleaned. But she didn't have time.

The wound on her arm was jagged, and as she sat up she saw how much she'd bled into the sand...until she'd died. She remembered holding it before her face as she leapt through the window on the third floor. She looked up at the shattered window.

Felt her face. There were wounds on her face. Her shirt, a simple blue cotton work-a-day thing, was torn, and there were deep wounds on her shoulder and down her back. One calf, too, had been cut by the glass. Glass and shards of wood from the sash windows littered the sand around her, like she'd been making angels at Christmas, only in broken glass.

She knew her life was a gift. It was impossible to imagine what it had cost her son to give it to her, because she'd been dead a hundred times over, from breaking her neck, to the fall, to the blood loss.

Any one of those things should have made her weak and useless, but somehow Jonathan's touch invigorated her. The knowledge that it wasn't over leant her strength...and her rage, too.

Yes, she thought, holding that rage inside. Anger, pure and simple, because that sick fucker had her baby.

'Thank you, darling boy,' she told Jonathan. He smiled, pleased. 'Let's go.'

But Jonathan shook his head.

You're on your own, he seemed to be saying.

'No, baby...don't...don't go...'

But already he was fading. She felt tears welling up again and this time she swallowed them. She didn't have time to cry for Jonathan or David or Marc.

Franklin would be taking Sam to the Black Room and she had work to do before she could follow down the long road to the bastard's final death.

*

The hooks through Paul's flesh didn't hurt anymore. He hung, remembering. Not *reminiscing*, which seemed like a pleasant way to remember, but remembering his fingers inside a cat.

As a young boy he remembered putting his fingers into the cat and touching it somewhere inside. Maybe it had been the cat's spine, or some nerve bunch. He'd touched it and it had danced and Franklin had laughed, but he'd been complicit, hadn't he?

He was complicit, still.

It was all his fault. He could see that now. He could still feel terror, though he was too far gone into his hypersanity to feel it on the surface, but it was his fault and he didn't doubt the terror or the blame that lay with him.

Complicity. One time, any one time, if he'd have stood and been a man none of this would have happened.

You were but a boy, a voice said. He didn't know to whom the voice belonged, but it sounded just like his own.

Some part of him understood that as much as he told himself he wasn't insane with fear, he couldn't deny it when he heard footsteps above. Of course it was Franklin.

He remembered the cat. His fingers in the cat.

You think that's the worst I've ever done?

A hatch, like into a basement, opened above. Paul understood where he was. Where he'd been for the past two days.

In his old house, in the fens, Cambridgeshire.

Somewhere new, under the house, that hadn't been there when their Dad was alive, when they'd both grown up together. Franklin had built the Black Room for his experiments, and he'd got better with practice.

Just how much, Paul was about to find out.

'Franklin! You fuck!' he said when Franklin's foot hit the first rung of the ladder leading down. He thought he roared, but his voice was cracked and the words came out as a mere whisper.

The agony from the hooks was too much for him. Even the effort of trying to shout tore more blood from him.

Don't pass out, he told himself, but already the lightness in his head was too much, then he was gone for a time.

*

There was no magic bullet to kill the dead. Irene knew this as she packed. She packed some baby things, because she also knew, completely and without a shadow of a doubt, that whatever happened she was coming home with her baby.

She wouldn't let Franklin take Sam. Turn him into himself, whatever the fuck he was doing. Sam was hers and not his, never would be. And she'd never let Franklin inhabit Sam to destroy him like he had David, and then Marc.

At the thought of her two dead friends – the best friends she'd ever had, a small sob escaped her lips. She punched the door jamb to wake herself up, because

134

crying would send her rage to sleep and let her sorrow rise up, then she'd lose.

She embraced the fresh pain and smiled. The smile would have been terrifying, had there been anyone to see it. Blood on her teeth, on her lips, a wound that still seeped in her scalp.

Irene swallowed the smile because she didn't like the way it felt on her lips. She needed the anger, but not too far. She strove for control and found it, somewhere deep down where her well of strength flowed.

She didn't go into the guest room, because she understood that the vision Jonathan had shown her was real. She didn't need to see David's mutilated corpse to know that it was true.

She didn't need to build on her anger. Already it was bubbling, running into her well, and it was rising.

But she needed to stay calm, for now.

'Slow down,' she counselled herself as she changed into fresh clothes. She couldn't do what she needed to in the torn and bloody clothes she'd died in. She was born anew now, and it felt fitting to put on fresh, clean clothes over the ragged mess of her body. That way, she could cover the worst of her wounds. She didn't want any questions. She didn't want any kind passerby to offer her aid.

What she needed to do, she could do alone. She needed to do it alone. This was between her and Franklin and she alone could finish it, because nobody else would understand. Nobody else *could* understand, that she had entrusted her child's life to her dead child...to Sam's brother.

So, instead of seeing David, and falling apart, she forced herself out of the house into the sea air. The air hit her and something washed away instantly. Her face relaxed and she let out a sigh.

'You can do this,' she said. 'Give me strength,' she added, but this time talking to the sea and not herself.

Then she nodded, set, and went into the small storage cabin around the front of the house. She took three things only.

A lighter Paul had hidden in a toolbox back when he'd pretended he didn't still smoke.

She took, too, a can of fuel.

Knives might be useless against the creature that now inhabited Marc's body. Maybe a gun, even if she'd had one, might be wasted. But if she burned him to death there'd be nothing he could do about coming back.

God help him, she'd burn him to cinders.

Just in case, though, she took a 5 kilo sledgehammer, too. Heavy, but not so heavy she couldn't swing it.

Even a corpse couldn't do much with two broken legs. Least, that's what she figured. If it came down to it, though, she'd rather burn him and be sure.

She understood perfectly what it would take to get Sam back. No reasoning. Nothing mortal. No worrying about the police, or legality, or talking.

She had to slaughter Franklin and make sure he could never come back. She needed to destroy him utterly.

With one last look at the sea, she took a deep breath and held that crisp pure smell in her memory for later. She thought she might need it.

'I'll be back,' she told the sea. Tell it to the sea, she

thought. But she'd save that for later, when Sam was home.

She'd beat him. She didn't doubt it for a second, because she was a mother, and Sam was hers.

*

Irene opened the door to the boathouse, the old damp wood creaking as she slid the doors aside.

Marc's boat was gone.

Hers was in the sea.

She didn't scream, cry, swear. She just nodded. Of course it would be. Franklin didn't make mistakes, but this time he had, because he'd thought she was dead, and her son, Sam's brother, his twin, had brought her back to life.

She turned away from the boathouse and walked along the sand, along the point, along the spit, toward the mainland and Marc's car...but of course, Marc's car would be gone. But she'd find it and with it she'd find Sam.

She knew he wasn't dead.

She'd find Franklin, too. He'd made a mistake. Like he'd made with Paul. He'd left her alive.

*

Paul came around slowly, like a man swimming up through the murky waters of a deep sleep. Franklin sat cross legged on the floor before him, looking up at him, a sick smile on his face.

'Feel any different?' he asked, grinning.

'Fuck you,' said Paul, though his voice was barely above a whisper. There was a disgusting taste on his tongue.

'The reflex to swallow when confronted with suffocation is as strong as the reflex to gag, you know. If you can't gag, that is. I held your mouth shut. I held your nose shut. You were unconscious. It's been more difficult in the past.'

'What...?'

Franklin flicked his head to the left. The door was to Franklin's right, to the left was the corpse. The man who'd been hanging was eviscerated. His eyes were gone, with nothing but bloody sockets left.

'What...?' croaked Paul, but he understood perfectly well.

His gag reflex worked just fine then.

'You sick...you sick fucker. I'm going to kill you.'

'No, Paul. I'm going to kill you, then I'm going to feed you to someone else. You see...'

'Fuck you!'

'No, Paul, fuck you. You took my girlfriend. You remember? She was mine.'

'You're sick, Frank. I can help...'

'I'm not sick. I'm a...scientist. You'll be my latest experiment. Immortality, Paul. Immortality.'

'I'll kill you.'

'You won't do a fucking thing! You understand? You're food, you...dippy...you're fucking food! I'm so close, Paul. Don't you get it? So close. You'll live on in another body. I can do it!'

Frank's eyes burned with insanity. Paul tried to sick it up, sick it out, the parts of the body he'd been forced to eat, but he couldn't. He was too dry. He imagined Frank feeding him small morsels, rubbing his throat like when they used to get their cat to eat his worming tablets, before Frank killed it.

Of course, Paul remembered it all now...Mr. George's cat. Their cat. The missing dogs. The spate of horse mutilations...

How many animals?

How many people?

How many people, Paul? How many people because you'd been too scared to say anything? Too fucking afraid, and now you're paying for it with your life.

'I'm going to have to leave you. Just for a short time. I need another subject. I'll be back. You see, I'm going to try to feed you to Irene. Seems poetic, somehow. I don't think it'll work, because men into women doesn't seem to take...'

'You bastard...'

'I'll be back. Be a good boy, dippy. I'll be back.'

That little thing, that pet name, was the goad Paul needed, not the thought of Irene, but the thought of the innocence Frank had stolen so long ago. The thought of his own part in this, knowing Frank was sick and never doing anything about it.

Frank pushed himself up and turned to go and Paul's rage and terror and yes, his shame, ignited.

*

With his lips curled back in a snarl that split his lips bloody, Paul swung himself up just as Franklin turned his back. With a dry scream he *willed* himself through the agony, forward, and then back, then forward, like on a child's swing. On the way forward the next time he tore the hooks from his flesh, taking off his first and second knuckles from each hand, and the fingers. His weight, swinging, tore the hooks from the meat of his back, his thighs, his calves. Blood splashed from his hands across the room.

Franklin swung back around... 'Fuck...!' he shouted and punched Paul in the face, breaking his nose and his cheek, as he was falling. Franklin was fast, much faster than Paul.

But Paul could see everything now, now that he was through insanity and out the other side.

He could see he was dead. He'd known he was dead but for his heartbeat the first time he woke in this nightmare pit.

But Irene wasn't dead. She wouldn't be. He wouldn't let it happen. He was dead, but he'd make his death count. He'd make sure she lived. She had to live. She had to...

And so did his children.

Franklin aimed a kick at Paul's ruined legs, but Paul threw himself into an embrace, the only thing he could do, and bit into Franklin's neck. Franklin's hold loosened and his hand went to his throat. Then Paul elbowed him in the face and heard a loud wet crack. Maybe Franklin's own cheekbones snapping under the force.

Franklin fell to the floor. Blood poured from the

wound in his neck. His eyes rolled in his head, then Paul could see the whites as Franklin passed into unconsciousness.

Paul could feel his own life leaving him. His blood poured in torrents from his wounds. In minutes, maybe, he would be unconscious, like Franklin.

He didn't have time to kill his brother, and he couldn't, even now. Couldn't bring himself to finish it.

But someone else could finish it. And he could still save Irene and his unborn children...those beautiful children he'd never know. But he'd give his life gladly for any one of them.

He left Franklin unconscious and bleeding on the floor.

Paul was lost, but if he could just get out of the house...if he could die somewhere close by...people would look. They'd come back. It would end.

Blood poured from his maimed hands and he slipped time and time again, trying to climb the ladder to the hatch.

His head swam as he climbed. He wanted to lie down, die. Wanted death, because the pain was immense, right there behind his sanity, waiting for him.

He fought it, fought the ladder, climbed, flipped open the hatch.

He stumbled through his childhood home, barely seeing all the small things that should have brought warm memories, but he could think of nothing except making it to the front door.

With his hands next to useless, his legs buckling as he walked, he made it to the front door.

He pulled it open and wandered with his eyes closing, opening, closing...

Wandered, on the cusp of death, into the road that ran through the wide flat fens and into the path of an oncoming lorry.

*

Paul died on impact.

It took only a half hour for the police to arrive on the scene.

'Fuck,' said the first policeman.

The second policeman threw up in Paul's old front garden, right next to Paul's head.

The ambulance arrived two minutes later. The paramedics had seen worse, but not by much. Neither slept well that night, and one, a man called Peter Jones, quit his job three months later. It wasn't because of Paul, but because of what they found down below, in the Black Room.

Paul's childhood neighbours stood and talked to the police, pointing at the house from which Paul had emerged. The police found the door still open. A smell escaped the house that both officers had smelled before, a smell of death. They followed their noses and made their careers through a fluke when they found the Black Room, and ended one promising young paramedic's career for good.

Franklin wasn't dead. Curled in a ball, he was covered in his own blood. For a time, the police and the paramedics discussed what had happened. The subject of leaving the man to die came up...but they couldn't be sure which one was responsible, or if it was both, or neither.

If they'd known for sure, would they have done it? Left him to bleed out?

The man called Peter Jones wished he had. He'd wanted to. That was why he quit. Because he wanted to kill whoever was responsible for what had happened in the Black Room, and when he knew he could have, he couldn't live with it.

22 people died in the Black Room, as near as the police could eventually figure. Paul died on the road, but it would have been 23. Peter Jones never could live with what he'd failed to do.

It should have been 24. But Franklin was given 22 life sentences. It should have been enough, but it wasn't. It never is.

*

When dawn was long gone, Irene reached the mainland and the car park by the docks.

Her feet were sore. She wore sensible boots, but even then, she couldn't stop the sand getting in between her feet and her socks. Her feet bled, but she didn't mind the pain. She'd felt worse. Still did. Her cuts hurt and she knew she had sand in those, too. They'd fester if she didn't do something about them, but she didn't have time. She could feel Sam calling her, feel his need, in her belly and her heart and her chest. Her breasts were full and tight because he was long overdue a feed. They hurt, too, and somehow that was the worst of her pains, because it was a pain only a mother could know.

Sam was waiting. He needed her and she needed him more than she'd ever known a mother could.

But first, she needed a car.

She didn't know a damn thing about stealing cars, other than the fact that if you don't know how to steal a car the next best thing is to have the keys.

She walked around the car park, checking tourists' cars for any that were unlocked first. All the tourists would be out with the dawn to see the seals. The first time she'd come to Blakeney she'd done the same, oohed and aahed at the seals, loved the feel of the boat rocking beneath her, the feeling of the sea spray in her hair and on her face, feeling refreshed afterward.

She wanted Sam to grow up with that love, embraced not only by his mother, but by the whole of the sea, too. To nurture him in Blue House became her reason for going on, for a time, before his birth. Now, she still wanted it, but she knew Blue House, any house...the house didn't matter. She wasn't doing this for a house. She was doing it for her son.

Going to sacrifice herself?

No. Don't think like that, honey.

No, she thought. The voice was right. She was going to kill, not to die.

Irene nodded to herself and pushed her hair around her face again, covering the worst of her wounds. The last thing she needed was some helpful passerby trying to get her an ambulance. God, she sure as hell looked like she needed one.

She headed into the car park after dropping off a couple of her essentials, checked the passenger doors on any cars she passed, walking in what she hoped was a casual manner. She only checked passenger doors because she figured most cars had central locking, and someone checking passenger seats looks less suspicious than someone checking a boot or a driver's seat.

A woman with a baby carrier the least suspicious of all.

The sledgehammer and the can of fuel didn't fit the image she wanted to show anyone looking. She left those at the side of the boathouse to pick up if she could get a car.

A woman with a torn scalp and numerous lacerations, walking like she was in agony, didn't help either, but she couldn't do anything about that but let her hair fall across her face and hope no one was about.

She found two cars that hadn't been locked, but there were no keys.

The third she checked under the driver's seat, too, because that was where she would have put her keys if she didn't want to carry them. Maybe if she'd been worried about dropping them in the sea. Probably a woman, she thought. A man was more likely to have pockets and keep his keys on him. A woman would take a handbag, but maybe someone who was a little impractical, hadn't prepared. The kind of woman who takes a small handbag and wears heels to go walking in the hills. The kind of girl who drove a Beetle, or a Mini, maybe.

The first Mini she came to she checked under the

driver's seat. Out of sight, but easy to get to. She hit gold.

Stealing a car, it turned out was easy.

Perhaps it'd be the easiest thing she did all day.

She scooted over into the driver's seat and arranged the seat and the mirror for herself, shorter than the woman who's car she was about to steal. The car was new and started first time. She took a second too check over the controls, look at the dash, and familiarise herself with an unfamiliar car.

Then she pulled out slowly, like it was the simplest thing in the world to steal someone else's car. She drove over the bump, shingle surface of the car park nice and slow, too, trying not to drive with the urgency she felt. It wouldn't do to attract attention, now she was so close to being on the road to the Black Room and the end.

Irene stopped for a second beside the boathouse and put the can of fuel and the sledgehammer in the passenger's foot well. Then she turned south and began the long drive to the fenlands of Cambridgeshire. To Paul and Franklin's family home.

To the Black Room.

*

The back roads of Norfolk wound and twisted enough to get tourists lost. There were hardly any road signs, but Irene knew these roads. It was where she was raised, and her sense of direction didn't fail her.

But she did feel woozy...no sleep but death, a broken neck, all her wounds, the blood loss...she was in trouble after an half an hour, and after an hour she knew she wouldn't make the journey without food and drink. Some strong coffee, some chocolate.

Her breasts were throbbing worse than all her wounds. For a moment she wondered if she could somehow relieve the pain that was building. It seemed the nearer to Sam she got the worse the urge to feed became...but it might have been because she'd been away from her baby for so long.

She checked the clock on the dashboard and realised it was already afternoon. Afternoon, late autumn, she had no chance of making it to the fens before darkness fell.

Maybe that was for the best. She thought about it, and realised her best chance was to get to Paul and Franklin's old house in the dark, so she could park unseen down the street.

But first she needed fuel. She'd lost a lot of blood, and even though her wounds were sealed tight with scabs and sand, her weakness would just continue to get worse.

She pulled over at a roadside petrol station, a small thing that sold red diesel for tractors, with no CCTV in the forecourt. Then she realised she didn't have any money.

Would the woman who left her keys in her girl's car have left some money?

She thought maybe she would have. Some change, for parking, for trolleys. That kind of thing. She checked the glove compartment and found nothing, but hit the jackpot when she checked the door pockets. A bottle of water and a small purse full of change and two twenties.

The fuel gauge was still on half full – it had barely

moved since she began driving.

Just fuel for her, she thought.

Eat and drive, honey, said a voice in her head. *It's got to end tonight.*

She knew the voice made sense.

There were stands in the petrol station with two for one on high caffeine drinks. She took four, and two sandwiches, and three bars of chocolate.

The clerk handed over her change. He didn't say anything about her wounds, and she kept her head down, but she could sense him looking. She tried to ignore it. Took her change without saying anything but thanks and got into the car and began the next stretch of the journey. Out of Norfolk and into the wide treeless expanse that was the fens.

*

After the winding roads of Norfolk, the long roads of the fenlands were a relief for a time, until they too felt like they went on forever, on and on into an unchanging and darkening horizon. Tiredness seeped into Irene's eyes. She fought to stay awake despite three cans of high caffeine drink that she'd taken.

It was a lonely drive down. A long way down south. Four hours along crappy country roads with nothing to do but drive and think. She drove from memory. She didn't need a map to hit the fens. It was easy enough. Once she was there she'd never forget where to go.

She had no one to talk to but herself.

She didn't want to, though, so she talked to Paul

instead and pretended he was right there in the car with her.

'Hey baby,' she said, looking to her left. She could see him there. He hadn't shaved, and his feet were bare. He had one hairy foot on the dashboard, like he was totally relaxed. His toenails, she saw, needed cutting.

'Honey. I've missed you.'

'I miss you,' she said. She reached across the gearstick and touched his leg, just to feel him, solid, beautiful. His feet smelled a little, from wearing trainers without socks, like he always did.

It was a good smell.

He smiled at her. One of his teeth was misaligned though the one that Franklin had knocked out was still there. His teeth had some stains on them from smoking, too, that he just couldn't brush out. She didn't mention it. She never had, because he'd pretended he'd given up smoking for her and that was good enough. Anything and everything he did was always good enough, and sometimes a hell of a lot better.

'You know this can't end well, don't you?'

She nodded. She knew it. He didn't have to ruin it and point it out.

'I'll get Sam back,' she said.

'I know you will, honey. I know you will.'

'I'm sorry, Paul,' she said after another few miles of driving, silence in the car, but a sweet silence full of things that didn't need to be said.

'I know,' he said. 'But it wasn't your fault. It was just a stupid accident.'

'I lost our baby,' she said. 'I can't make up for that.'

149

'Get Sam back, then,' he said. 'If you make a mistake, if you're wrong, you better be damn sure and make it right.'

She smiled, just a small sad smile that didn't touch her eyes. But she knew he was right.

'I'm not sorry you fought him, you know. I used to think...used to think...what happened to you...'

'It's OK. I'm a big boy.'

She nodded. Drove on for a while. They talked for another hour or so. The journey flew by with him to talk to. He'd always been good company.

She might have cried while she talked, but it might have just been the tiredness. After all, she hadn't slept all night. She'd just been dead.

Paul laughed when she told him that one. He had a good laugh.

She drove on and on, sometimes quiet, sometimes talking. Then she looked to her left and he wasn't there anymore.

*

The street was a long, wide stretch of road with no spot to park, or pull over. She wanted to park down the street, take her time, walk up and check things out before she went in to the house.

She could have parked in the road, like Franklin used to, back when she'd dated him. But she was worried about someone sounding their horn at her, even though the road was quiet. The horn might alert Franklin that she was there.

Did it matter if he knew she was coming?

Would he be slow? Slow now that the decay in Marc's dead body had advanced?

Franklin had told her that close to the mannequin, that vile thing that thump thump thumped with the heart of him, he told her that he could survive in a body for longer.

Had he flown to Spain to kill his mother and taken the mannequin with him? She thought he had. He would have had to.

Just how long could he survive in a body, just how strong would he be with the focus of his power close by?

She had to believe that as a dead man he would be slower. Weaker. Weak enough for her to fight? To win? To burn him down, and that evil mannequin, too?

She realised she didn't have a choice but to get on with it.

'Get to it, honey,' said Paul, even though he wasn't there.

Her only option was to park on Paul's old house's drive.

She pulled into the driveway with her lights off. She couldn't do anything about the sound of the tires on the gravel driveway, but she didn't need to make too much of a show of arriving.

She had no idea whether Franklin had seen her already.

She couldn't take the chance that he hadn't.

She took the sledgehammer from the passenger seat, rather than the fuel. She could burn it down once he'd broken him.

Irene took a few steadying breaths. Then she pulled the handle, stepped out in the brisk night air. She left the driver's side door ajar, because she didn't need to make the noise it would just to shut it.

Could she really do it? Could she beat him?

It didn't matter, she knew. There was no one else, and she'd never trust another living soul to do what she needed to. She would have trusted Paul, or Marc, even, but they were dead, weren't they?

She had to trust in herself. She hefted the sledgehammer over her shoulder, ready to swing.

She could see through the stained glass in the front door into the hallway beyond. Stained glass that Paul had told her Franklin had once broken, pushing him up against it in a childish fight, back when they were teenagers.

The hallway was empty.

She tried the handle. The front door was unlocked. It opened with a swish, a small rug behind it pushed back by the base of the door.

She put both hands back on the sledgehammer and walked into Franklin's lair.

*

Franklin was in the house somewhere, she knew, because she could...smell him? Sense him?

No. It was that smell. Shit and rot. Putrescence and sickness. Yellowing flesh and failing bodies.

Marc rotting. Rotting until Franklin could perform his transformation and steal another body.

She had to face the fact that she wouldn't be getting Marc back. Never.

Her beautiful friend who she'd met for the first time when she interviewed him. Her beautiful friend who in such a short time had become so dear to her.

The last time she'd see her friend would be when she smashed his face in with a sledgehammer. After that she wouldn't see him ever again, because she'd douse him in petrol, flick Paul's lighter to his decaying corpse, and burn him to ashes.

She left the front door open behind her. With the sledgehammer at the ready, perfectly capable of smashing her best friends face, knowing that he wasn't her friend any longer, Irene Jacobs walked down the hall, following her nose. That stench was strong.

He's down there, in the Black Room. Black with dried blood, she thought. *Where Paul died.*

But Franklin wasn't in the Black Room.

She heard his soft footsteps a moment too late to turn, that sickening stench becoming stronger at the last second as he rushed her with surprising speed for a dead man. Speed she hadn't expected and wasn't prepared for.

He punched her in the back of the head and lights exploding in her vision. She sagged down, even though she fought it. He caught her in a strong hand around her throat. She gagged because he cut off her wind. Then he jabbed a needle into her neck and pumped her full of sedative.

*

153

Her whole family were there in the Black Room. A family of the dead, a grotesquery, a tableau of slaughter.

Jonathan sat on Irene's lap. Her baby looked up at her, no longer a toddler but just a little baby. His lips were blue. He had livor mortis on his back, livid purple and full of dead blood. Around his neck was a thick knot of flesh where he'd been strangled by an umbilical cord.

He'd been born dead, killed because of her stupid accident, or maybe he'd been dead before. It didn't matter.

Yes, yes it does, someone said, but nobody's mouth moved.

Paul was there, smashed to pieces, missing an arm and a leg...the pieces he'd lost when a lorry hit him. His face was barely recognisable, but for some reason he was naked and she recognised what remained of his body. His head sat in his lap and he held it there with his remaining hand. The first two fingers of his hand were missing, too. His hand slipped, and his head tumbled to the floor, but there was no sound in the...

Dream. Dream of us 'til you wake. You have to wake.

Marc and David were rotten blotted corpses, holding hands. Marc was light, ethereal, almost transparent. David bore the wounds he had after death, in some sick twist of fate, doomed to spend the rest of eternity a husk, blind in whatever fucked up afterlife this was.

You're here, too, Irene. Remember?

Her mother walked up to her, seemingly fine, until she tried to make a sweet noise at baby Jonathan. Irene realised her throat had been cut from ear to ear. The sweet baby noise came out as a gurgle, and blood

154

splattered across her and the baby.

Irene just smiled and wiped the blood from the baby's eyes, happy because her family was with her at last.

But where's Sam, Irene. Where's Sam?

'I thought I'd never see you all again,' she said.

But no one could talk, because they were dead, weren't they? They couldn't come back, but she could.

Then whose voice was she hearing? Who was whispering in her ear?

In her dream she could feel the pain from her limbs and from her back. Such pain that she could not bear. She was drawn from her position, where she'd been sitting. Drawn high.

Jonathan grew, though, to a toddler's size as she realised she was no longer sitting, but hung, swinging from hooks. Her arms were pulled back, stretching her shoulders painfully, and the toddler dropped from her arms to the floor. He pushed himself up and swung her, chuckling, while she screamed in agony from the hooks in her flesh. He pushed her like she would have done for his giggles on a child's swing.

Paul came and pushed from behind, somehow able to find his way and push even though he was decapitated, mutilated almost beyond recognition. She cried out in pain, in terror, in sorrow...but the dead did not care, her dark family just pushed all the harder.

David and Marc and her mother all pushed and she swung and screamed until she woke and found that the dream was true.

She hung from the hooks and Marc pushed her back and forth, smiling, grinning, with missing teeth and rotting lips.

'Awake?' he said. 'Good.'

He pulled a knife from his pocket and flicked it open. He held it before her eye.

'Scream all you like. No one can hear you down here.'

He cut off her right ear, and she did scream. She screamed until her throat was raw.

*

'You know, I always wondered what it'd be like. Hanging there. I never took a body from here. I think I'm going to have to take one soon, though. Marc's not up to much. Your queer boy friend's falling apart on me.'

He spoke into her ear, which he held in his hand. Blood ran in a heavy river down the side of Irene's neck and onto her shirt, a blue cotton shirt that looked black in the heavy light and the blood.

'I'm going to kill you,' she managed, through such agony she never knew existed.

'I don't think you are,' he said. He laughed, insane and cheerful.

'I'm going to get my baby back,' Irene managed, though the pain, towering, immense, threatened to pull her back under, into a dream populated by the dead.

Sam hadn't been in the dream because he wasn't dead. *He's not dead.*

Just knowing that gave her the strength to smile at the madman holding her ear.

It gave him pause for a second. She saw rage and confusion flicker across his face.

Not yet.

She let the smile sink down, confused herself. She was dying, probably, or would soon be dead. And yet she wanted to smile. Maybe she'd been driven insane, with the pain and sorrow. Maybe she was as insane as Franklin.

'He's upstairs. I don't think he likes me. You can see him soon. He'll be down here, in your place, though,' he said. 'I'll keep him down here, 'til he's big enough, anyway. I'll probably need a few bodies by then. Even with the mannequin close by, I'll need a few more bodies. Fifty? A hundred? I confess, Irene, I don't really know. Still, easy enough to get them. It's not like there's a shortage of people.

'But I think I'll fuck with you a little while, first.'

'Fuck you,' she spat. For some reason there was blood in her spit, too, and she felt a piece of tooth come flying out. She'd bitten down so hard against the pain she'd cut her mouth and cracked her own teeth.

'No, honey,' he said, and that hurt more than the hooks and the gaping hole where her ear had been, because it was what Paul used to call her. 'I am going to kill you. But I don't want to waste the chance to have a little fun.'

Her sledgehammer was in the corner. He saw her looking at it.

'That? You think you can get it?'

No. She didn't. But she couldn't let him win.

'No.'

'I can, because I'm not hanging from hooks, see?'

He held out his hands and wriggled his fingers.

157

'Let's play, shall we?'

He walked to the corner of the room. Picked up the sledgehammer and she knew she'd lost.

Not yet, said that voice. *Not yet.*

Paul? Didn't sound like Paul. But either way, all it did was make things worse, because there was no hope. Sam was alive, but she'd lost. There was no way to win.

Pain to come, but no more sorrow, unless it followed her in death. She knew she was going to die now, and she'd been fooling herself to ever think she could do anything else against Franklin.

'Sorry,' she said, for Sam, for all the dead that came because she'd fallen in love with Paul. But she couldn't be sorry for that. Not ever, not even with Sam upstairs, beyond her hearing, even though she could feel him. Not even with Franklin coming at her with her sledgehammer, the one she'd fooled herself into thinking would smash him to pieces. But it was her that was going to feel its dull bite.

'Sorry,' she said again, and cried, her tears mixing with her blood, as he came at her.

*

'Let's play a little game,' he said while she sobbed. She didn't want to beg but she would. Anything so he didn't do it.

'Please,' she said. 'I'll do anything...I'll...'

He swung the hammer. Broke her shin. She screamed and screamed and then blacked out again.

'Fuck,' she heard him say as she drifted

under...consciousness, wakefulness, was a murky pool, and she felt herself sinking, sinking to the bottom.

As though from under thick scum filled water, she heard the hatch to the Black Room open and shut. She tried to swim back to consciousness, but she couldn't.

For a time, she closed her eyes and there was nothing, no thought, no pain, no love or anger or sorrow. Just...nothing...

And then, they came to her and pulled her up.

*

Her family were there again, her rotten and dead family. In one instant they were pulling her through murky crud filled water and out into the air. Even though she knew it was just a dream before death, she still took a deep breath before she opened her eyes and looked around.

She wasn't beside a pool, in the open air. She was in the Black Room, still.

She wanted to cry, but you can't cry in a dream, you can't cry when you're hanging from rusted iron meat hooks looking down at the ruins of your ear on the floor and your body, swinging, surrounded by a morbid family gathering of mutilated dead. They swung her and swung her and though she understood now the pain to come she couldn't wake, the pain was too much.

But it wasn't that they were being malicious. Paul, her beloved, looked infinitely sad, his head looking up from below, even though he stood behind and pushed. Jonathan, giggling, a toddler still, pushed her backward. Her mother, whom she'd never particularly liked, looked upon her with love, too.

Marc and David held hands in this sick dream, and pushed at her with their free hands, pushed so hard that she swung like a small child on a swing, back and forth at an insane tempo, the agony from her limbs and her back growing and growing...

'Wake up,' someone said.

That voice she didn't know. It was none of her family. Not Jonathan, either. She knew Jonathan's voice well enough, even though he would never speak.

'Wake up!'

No, no, no, she wanted to say, but the pain of swinging on the hooks was too much...too much. The only way to stop them swinging her was to wake...

To wake...

She woke, but there was no one there but her and the only person who could save Sam was her.

She swung, still, from the dead pushing her in her dream. She put her own effort into it too, growling and biting down so hard she cracked her own jaw bone.

Back and forth, *swing, swing, honey*, and that was Paul's voice, in her head, driving her on before she passed out again because agony was her friend now and she knew how Paul got down from the hooks.

Because he loved enough to take the pain. So did she. She swung, growling, blood pouring, flesh tearing, until she felt the hooks in her flesh pulling away, taking her flesh with them, and then she tore her back free completely. Her top half came free, the hooks ripping though her triceps first, then the weight of her upper body tearing the hooks from her hands, in between the

160

flesh of her carpal bones, from the big trapezius muscles in her back, but leaving her legs hooked. She fell straight to the floor, not expecting it, not expecting it at all, and smashed her head into the black concrete floor.

She swam down again, saying '*no, no,*' over and over again.

The pain was too much, but her family were there, pushing her, pulling her, trying to get her free.

Jonathan, a toddler again, sat on his haunches and stroked her hair from her face.

'Why?' she asked, from within the dark.

But she might as well have asked the sea.

And while she sank down, the dead pulled on her ruined legs. Pulled hard enough to tear the last of her flesh free.

*

Irene came around from unconsciousness again, and her legs were free of the hooks. There was a fire in her limbs, something burning bright, and she remembered it was pain, but it was a kind of pain that had become part of her. She couldn't walk, because he'd completely shattered her shin, but she could crawl. She crawled to the corner, under the stairs and took up the sledgehammer in her torn hands.

It was her one chance. Her only chance. She knew she'd never get another.

If you've made a mistake, if you've done something wrong, you better make damn sure you make it right.

'Paul...' she said, but her dead had deserted her now

she was awake. She missed them. Wounds and all. But now she was like them. She was no longer whole. She raised her hand to the side of her head, but then she let her hand dropped again.

The loss of an ear didn't fucking matter.

He mattered. The sledgehammer. Sam.

Nothing else. Nothing else in the whole world but this moment and this place and this one last chance.

She willed herself to stillness. Willed her hands to work on the sledgehammer, though they were slipping even on the rubber grip, slick with blood. The first two fingers on her right hand wouldn't work, and she couldn't stand. There was a fire in the side of her head and she was groggy from the blood loss. She could feel the break in her leg, a part of the pain, a scene in the whole of a movie, but she shut it down, concentrated on the smiling faces of her family, because suddenly they were back, just as dead, but she wasn't alone down here in the dark.

Then she realised it wasn't dark. The light was still on.

*

He was coming. She heard his footsteps sounding out on the floorboards above. The light...a bulb hanging from the ceiling. He'd know. Of course. He'd see the space where she should have been hanging and he'd see her under the stairs and he'd know.

But he came down the stairs and her family were there. Her family were always there, dead or alive.

'Fuck,' he said. 'How...'

She heard his feet crashing on the stairs as he ran down quickly in heavy boots.

The light bulb dimmed momentarily as he stepped onto the last stair.

'Bitch,' he said, and turned, because he knew exactly where she was.

But when the light went out and it became pitch black she remembered exactly where he was and he was disoriented. He didn't see her or the sledgehammer as she slammed it down onto his foot.

*

She heard the crunch and then a scream, thought of Marc, but only for a second. Of course he hadn't screamed – he felt no pain.

But she could destroy him. She didn't need his pain.

She hit out again, missed, then threw herself forward and swung again, this time catching his knee cap as he fell to the floor.

She was screaming the whole time, her throat already raw. Spittle flew from her mouth, and for a time, she wasn't dead or alive, but in that space in between that few ever get to see. A space where there is light in darkness, over beyond the borders of sanity. Paul had known that place.

Irene was there as she swung the hammer again.

The light came on and he reached for her, but even from her crouch she could swing hard enough to break his shoulder, then his face. She swung again and again, until he could stand no more.

163

She pulled herself away from her friend's broken body, but the creature on the hard stone floor was no longer recognisable as her friend.

'You fucking bitch,' said Franklin, his words slurred. But he wasn't a threat now. He was just a lump of hammered meat.

She stood back, ignoring his words.

She thought that maybe he spoke while she worked, but she wasn't sure. At that point she heard so many voices it might as well have been silent.

She might not have been able to stand, but then, neither could he. She made sure, though. She broke every limb, screaming from her own pain and rage as she swung the hammer again and again.

There was hardly any blood because he was already dead.

She didn't have time to gloat, nor would she, because she couldn't stand to look at Marc's body, broken and shattered, there on the cold bloody floor of the Black Room.

'Finish it!' he shouted at her through the shards of his jaw and his teeth, but she was crawling up the stairs.

'Finish it!' he shouted again, and Irene felt a smile on her face. She didn't like the feel of that smile. It felt like it was coated in oil. But she couldn't shift it.

She left him the sledgehammer.

'Finish it yourself,' she said.

She flipped the hatch shut behind her.

*

Irene crawled through the house, dragging her shattered

164

leg behind her, leaving a trail of blood along the old unwashed carpet in the hallway. She followed the sound of baby Sam's wailing.

He was upstairs, screaming so loud she worried he would hurt himself.

She crawled up the stairs, each riser igniting fresh agony in her wounds. She was gushing blood from some of her wounds, still, but she wouldn't give in. Not now. Not when she was so close.

She felt her eyes slip shut at the top of the stairs, on the hallway landing, but Sam's screaming pulled her back awake.

She found him in Paul and Franklin's father's bedroom.

She thought she couldn't cry anymore, but she could. Sam was bellowing, a healthy wail. It wasn't a scream of distress, but because he was soiled and hungry – she understood that Franklin hadn't thought to feed Sam.

She was going to bleed to death, but she couldn't die. Not now. Not before Franklin was trapped forever.

She'd never make it to the car. She couldn't drive.

But she didn't need the fuel. She didn't need to burn the house down. No one knew he was there. She could just block up the passage, and leave him to rot. He'd never heal, and she knew why.

Because that stinking fucking mannequin was in the room and that was all she needed to finish this. She understood what it was. She understood why she heard the thump thump thump of a heartbeat every time she was near it.

It was his jar, his canopic jar, with the most important

165

organ of all inside.

*

She understood that it wasn't just his heart housed in the fucking thing, but his essence, his evil. It was that which stank, not the rotten heart, but the putrid nature of a man that had slaughtered more than twenty people, and a man who would kill and kill if she didn't finish it once and for all.

Marc's body was battered, destroyed, but could she guarantee he wouldn't find some way?

She smiled through cracked teeth at Sam and it seemed to calm him, though she wasn't sure he could actually see her well enough to tell a smile, but he knew his mother was in the room. His mum. She'd always be a mum to him. Never a mother.

That oily feel left her, and her smile was pure.

The sledgehammer was in the basement, in the Black Room. She knew she couldn't make it back down there. The fuel was in the car.

But the lighter was in her pocket. Paul's lighter.

She pushed against the mannequin and it teetered, but wouldn't fall.

She grabbed it around the steel base and yanked with all her strength, until the bastard thing fell with a heavy thump to the carpet.

For a moment she wondered what she'd do if the mannequin just wouldn't die.

But she didn't stop. She couldn't. Couldn't leave him any chance to come back, ever. It had to end now.

She could feel her blood still draining from her body. She slumped to the floor for a second and realised when she came too that she'd actually passed out.

'No.'

Sam was still crying. Maybe it was Sam that had stopped her slipping into death. Sam, holding her on, while the rest of her dead family just watched and waited. But this wasn't for them to finish. This was hers, and Sam's.

'Help me,' she said to no one in particular. The bastard mannequin seemed to laugh at her. The word SAM carved into its chest. She could imagine it rocking back upright, indestructible, the word SAM taunting her.

The heart within still beat. She could hear it reverberating through the room. Thump thump. Thump thump. Deafening, almost, in its intensity and power.

She couldn't burn the damn thing with just her lighter.

'Help me,' she said, and felt arms around her, pulling her up, holding her. She didn't have to look to know it was Paul.

He laid his good hand over hers. His good leg helped her bad one. Together they could end it.

Standing on one leg, borrowing Paul's strength. She tore the bedding from Paul's father's bed. Wrapped it around the mannequin, rolling it in the bedding, then Paul showed her what she needed. On the nightstand stood a bottle of aftershave.

Her smile was grim, and when she finally flicked the lighter at the mannequin, wrapped in old bedding, it took. It burned.

Then Paul lowered her to the floor next to Sam while

the mannequin burned and vile smoke filled the air.

*

Black fluid seeped from the mannequin and she heard Franklin scream in rage and terror from below. He felt it break. She knew it.

Flames licked across the carpet and up the wooden bed, spreading fast. The smoke was filling the room, now, sickening and pungent.

Paul was right there, giving her strength, though part of her knew he was a long time dead and it just couldn't be. But like a crutch to her, behind her, holding her sitting but so she couldn't see how badly he'd been mutilated, he helped her, dragging her and Sam down the stairs. She gritted her teeth against the pain and strove on, pushing herself on her arse where she had to.

And she smiled as her blood poured, with baby Sam, because if she was going to die, she wanted him in her arms.

Upstairs, the flames roared.

Downstairs, Irene Jacobs, nee Harris, crawled through the open front door, underneath the smoke, to the fresh air.

She freed herself from her shirt and Sam latched on. With a smile on her face she waited to see if she would die

For a second, drifting, there on the front path, she thought she heard the thump thump thump of Franklin's black heart within the mannequin.

But it was only broken fists on the burning hatch door

PART FOUR
THE BLUE HOUSE (II)

On a hard cold Christmas Eve, Irene Jacobs sat on the shore out on the point, staring out to a black sea she could barely see in the lights coming from the Blue House behind her.

Tell it to the sea, she thought. That was easy though.

She heard footsteps, light, on the sand.

Tell it to your eleven year old son, though? That was hard. Explain to him why you were missing an ear. Why you limp badly, and heavily in the cold and wet. Explain to him where his father went, why no one ever comes out to visit the Blue House?

How do you explain all that to your eleven year old son?

Go through the borders of sanity, to the last moments of your life when you should have died, and the dead picked her up and took her and Sam out into the road away from the fire that raged through the old house, gutting it completely from the eaves right down to the basement. How no bones were ever found down there in the basement, no ruined corpse. Or where a car she'd stolen had just disappeared to. She never did know if it was found. She hoped so.

How? How do you tell all that to anyone, let alone your sole flesh and blood. Your sole family. Your reason for being alive and wishing to continue being alive for as long as it took.

Same as you told it to me, the sea seemed to say. She smiled and took strength from it.

'Sam,' she said. 'Sit with me a while.'

At the beginning, she figured. That's where you started.

'Sam,' she said. 'Have I ever told you how I met your father?'

'No,' he said, and she was struck by just how like that voice she'd heard in the Black Room, guiding her, his voice was.

She smiled, and told it to her son, just like she'd told it to the sea, way back when, eleven years ago.

*

Christmas had always been a sad affair in the Jacobs household. For eleven years, it had been just the two of them. Sam and Irene. She'd made it as fun for him as she could.

It would have been a sad affair yet again, but things were different. She didn't know why or what was different in the twelfth year, but she felt it, felt something building inside her, like a big wave washing in from out to sea, washing the shore clear.

Irene was determined, filled with new vigour. She felt that she needed to make Christmas whole for the first time ever. She invited Sam's friends over on Christmas Eve for a party. She invited her employees from Beautiful Brides and their families. She invited Sam's friend's families.

The house was full for the first time in twelve years. She realised it felt good.

She smiled more than she had in public for twelve

years. She took a few drinks, handed round even more drinks. She felt comfortable among these people, and she realised that even those she did not know well did not stare at her scars, or question her on the events of the past. The gossip hounds of the small Norfolk coastal village had grown tired of gossiping with no basis in fact. She knew there were stories about her, about Sam, but she'd never joined in the gossip.

What had happened in the past remained in the past. It was between her and Sam and the dead.

She was having a good time, relaxed, free, smiling. Loose with her words and unguarded.

Smiling as she watched her son growing in among his friends, changing now he moved from small school to big school, shot up suddenly, turning into a tall teenager instead of a self-conscious young, small boy.

Confident. Beautiful. More like her than Paul, but she could see Paul in him, too, and more so as he became older.

She sat in a corner in her living room for a minute, feeling tired and not a little drunk, smiling and nodding as people came to check if she was OK.

The truth was, even though she was happy, she knew something was coming this night. She could almost feel it in the way the old pains woke in her wounds. Like she was awake again tonight, for the first time since Paul had died. Something was coming.

A wave to wash against the shore.

She sat, and drank, and waited until a knock came at the door. She excused herself and walked down the hall, limping heavily, into the lobby and opened the door.

Paul was there, and her mother. David and Marc. Jonathan, her sweet baby Jonathan.

It's time, they seemed to say.

She nodded and went back into the hallway and opened a credenza beside the back door. She took their remains that she had put there in the morning. Took them out, four urns only, held in a shopping bag.

Irene left the party behind her, and walked down to the sea in the dark.

*

Light from the house at her back lit her way down to the shore. Her family, her dead ones, followed her down.

She never did have Marc's ashes, but she knew why they'd come. This wasn't about the ashes. It was about letting go. Moving on. She'd been holding onto their love for her for the last twelve years. Holding onto their pain, cherishing the memories of their lives, yes, but taking that pain and bearing it like it was hers to own.

But it was not. It never was. It was not her fault that Franklin had killed all but Jonathan, and Jonathan was not her fault, either. It had been an accident.

Looking at her beautiful son now, she knew that, utterly, completely. She loved him. She did not want to let him go. He knew, as did the others, but it was time. Time for them to go.

She could not punish herself any longer. It was time to be reborn afresh. She bore wounds enough. She did not need to bear theirs, too.

Her mother kissed her on her cheek. She could swear

173

that she could feel that kiss, though her mother was nothing more than vapours in the cold winter's night.

'It's OK, honey,' said her mother. And for the first time in her life, Irene understood her mother. She hadn't been selfish, or immature. Just stunted...like Irene herself had become?

She didn't wonder if this revelation was true. She knew it to be so, just as she knew that her mother didn't want her to become the same as she had on her husband's death.

She kissed her mother in turn, and then emptied the ashes into the sea.

Her mother's vaporous ghost seemed to sigh, and then it drifted away on the wind.

David came to her next.

'I always loved you for what you were,' he said. The unspoken suggestion was that he loved her still, but not who she'd become.

He kissed her, too, and she nodded. Held his hand, solid enough for a ghost. She turned up the urn and watched one of her best friend's ashes taken away in the wind and the tide.

Marc came to her, said nothing. He smiled and stroked her hair. Tears came then, running down her face, and she could not help but remember the last time she'd seen his face, broken and battered with Franklin's insane eyes looking out at her.

But she understood his gift to her. His face now, looking down at her with a satisfied smile. Taking away that memory was his gift to her.

Jonathan came to her and snuggled into her hip. She

sat on the sand so that she could take him into her lap and hold him one last time, this solid boy who would have looked very similar to his brother, had he been given the chance to live.

But she had to let his soul loose, too. It wasn't held in the urn beside her in a shopping bag, but in her heart, and for her heart to be free she had to say goodbye to them all, these memories that had such weight.

She kissed his head, smelling his toddler's hair. He couldn't speak but to say no. He said it one last time, looking at her tears.

'No,' he said, and with his small hands wiped her tears away.

Irene sniffed and nodded, in turn, to her dead son. Then she emptied his ashes, too, into the sea and let them wash away.

At each passing, she felt unbearable lightness coming over her, like she too would float away as she let the weight fall from her shoulders.

All that was left was Paul. Silent, he sat beside her.

They sat that way for an hour. They spoke, comfortable, like twelve years hadn't passed since she'd seen him.

She stared out at the sea for a moment, feeling him there beside her, his shoulder touching hers. Then she turned to talk to him and he was gone.

*

That night Irene lay facing up, looking at the ceiling, the Blue House holding her tight.

175

The sea was in the house, a part of it, holding all her stories and whispering them through the open window in her bedroom.

Sam slept down the hall from her. Irene Jacobs lay alone, but for the Blue House and the memory of the dead.

But those memories were light, and comforted by them at last, she slept.

24th June 2011 – 16th August 2011

IF YOU ENJOYED
A HOME BY THE SEA,
CHECK OUT "RAIN" BY
THE SAME AUTHOR.

There was a brass bell above the door to John's bookshop. It didn't ring often.

Ting-ng.

Apart from Friday mornings. Then, it rang without fail.

"Morning, Mr. Hill," said John March, without looking up.

"John." Just that. No greeting. There never was.

John smiled to himself. He put the photograph he used as a bookmark between the pages of his book.

Mr. Hill walked up to the counter. He wouldn't use a stick, but he could have done with one. His old back was so bent that he was near enough walking at right angles.

He dumped two heavy bags onto the glass counter and sighed, rubbing at the angry red lines across the fat of his fingers.

Beneath the counter was a collection of first editions that really weren't worth much. John was more worried about the glass breaking than any damage to his books.

"Got a couple of bags … I don't know as you'd want 'em."

"I'll take a look. Let's see what you've got here."

John could have bought the lot of them in the charity shops for about a tenner. He knew full well that Mr. Hill had bought them for about the same.

It wasn't the point, though.

John March wasn't a local, but he wanted to make friends. It wasn't easy for an outsider to make a living with a bookshop in small-town Norfolk. Any friends he could make were worth their weight in gold.

Mr. Hill had been a customer in his first week, six months back. He came in every week. The fact that John hadn't made a single penny from their transactions wasn't the point. He wasn't even doing his civic duty, looking after the town's pensioners. Friends were hard to come by.

"How's Betsy?" asked John as he stacked the books on the

178

counter. He put the two hardbacks to one side. He'd never sell them. There were seventeen paperbacks. Each book in mint condition.

Mr. Hill seemed to think the condition of the book was the sole criterion for saleability.

"Farts all the time. Don't matter what I feed her. She just stinks."

"Maybe it's an allergy?"

"Nah."

John nodded. That's the way it goes, he thought. Sometimes you get a conversation. Sometimes you get one-liners, leaving you nowhere to go.

"Well," said John, pursing his lips, readying for the haggle, "I can give you two pounds for these." He laid a hand on the hardbacks. "Five pounds for the paperbacks."

"I was thinking ten for the lot."

"Ah, Mr. Hill. You know …"

"Don't tell me you don't sell the hardbacks. You've got plenty."

That's because nobody buys them, thought John, but he didn't say that.

"How about eight pounds for the lot?"

"I reckon they're worth at least a tenner."

John kept his face completely clear of expression. He just looked at Mr. Hill.

Mr. Hill went right on staring back at him.

John opened the till. Took out a tenner. Handed it to Mr. Hill.

Mr. Hill nodded.

"Thanks, John. I'll keep my eye out for some other good 'uns."

"I appreciate it."

Mr. Hill looked like he was going to say more. John didn't know if something was expected of him.

179

Mr. Hill didn't leave.

"You want to come out back for a coffee?"

A nod of a droopy face, and a small smile. Not really a smile. Just a hint of a smile, drifting past his eyes like a cloud passing the sun.

"Don't drink coffee. Plays me guts up. I left Betsy alone, though. She can't do the walk to town no more."

John nodded himself. He felt he'd done something right. He didn't know what, but Mr. Hill seemed pleased.

"I'll tell Mrs. Oldham about your shop. She likes a read."

"Thanks. I could always use the customer."

"She likes the old romances. Don't do anything for me. I like a western. The old war stories, too. I weren't old enough to fight in the war. My eldest brother did, though."

"He must have some stories."

"He's dead now."

Idiot. Mr. Hill didn't seem to mind, though.

"I've got some westerns, if you'd like to take a look."

"Maybe next time."

Every week, it was like an interview, or a test, except John didn't know the questions, or the answers, or the subject.

"Well, nice to see you."

"You too, John. Thanks. It's been a pleasure." Mr. Hill smiled at John. It was a warm smile.

Ting-ng.

Puzzled, John watched Mr. Hill walking down the alley past the big glass front. *It's been a pleasure.* He didn't know why the phrase struck him as odd. Maybe it was just because it wasn't the sort of thing Mr. Hill usually said. Normally he talked about his dog, Betsy, or his aching joints, or the weather.

Probably just freaked out because I got somewhere today, he thought. Trying to get the old man to buy a book was his current goal in life. He felt he'd come close today.

180

He put it from his mind, then sat down and picked up his book to pass the time.

Time was something he had plenty of.

"Chilling as an Arctic blast, Craig Saunders' bold and distinctive voice will haunt your dreams." - Bill Hussey, author of Through A Glass, Darkly and The Absence

RAIN

CRAIG SAUNDERS

CPSIA information can be obtained at www.ICGtesting.com
Printed in the USA
BVOW05s0204190914

367531BV00001B/5/P

9 780957 399914